The Requiem of Annie Ducayne

by

Terri McEachren- Levert

Library and Archives Canada catalogued this publication through Legal Deposit

McEachren-Levert, Terri L., 1971-, author
          The Requiem of Annie Ducayne/Terri McEachren-Levert

ISBN: 978-1-9992685-2-7 (softcover)

Published by: Reno Blue Productions, Chelmsford, ON P0M 1L0

Printed in Canada by OJGraphix

For the important people in my life:

Tyler and Kevin: my world. I simply couldn't live without you.

Mom and Dad: consistent, unwavering support. You waited a long time for me to create. I'm glad we can experience it together.

The rest of my family: we are a small tribe — but we will always have each other. Our family motto: "Everybody please just try to act normal!" ;p

Special thanks to Tyler, who went through every word in this book with me, helping me get unstuck, correcting weird word choices and talking about plot points until we were blue in the face – was a great time! His judgment was impeccable!

Special thanks to my first reader (L.J.), who didn't want any credit, but who helped in invaluable ways and showed me it was alright to let other people share in your gifts.

"If my devils are to leave me, I'm afraid my angels will take flight as well." Rainer Maria Rilke

"Find out the reasons that command you to write; see whether it has spread its roots into the very depth of your heart; confess to yourself you would have to die if you were forbidden to write."
Rainer Maria Rilke

Table of Contents

Years of Secrets

I

I died when I was 5.

Where did I go when I died? I must have went
somewhere. I try and try to figure it out, but the only
thing I can remember is blackness. Mother says I need to
forget about it, but I don't even remember what it was like
to be dead. Maybe I was floating in nothingness, maybe I
was happy and peaceful – or maybe I was terrified.
Perhaps the dark silence was lonely and suffocating.
Mother doesn't like it when I wake up screaming during
the night, but I have a lot of bad dreams. I never remember
them. They are gone the moment I open my eyes. I'm left
with a feeling of terror; blind fear without any idea of why.
It's distressing, and it happens often. At the beginning,
Mother used to run into my room in a panic to see what

was wrong, but the more it happened, the less she came to see. Now she just shouts an annoyed, "Go back to sleep," from the other room. I wish she would sit with me until I calm down, but she's not that kind of Mother. I learn to calm myself down, breathing in through my nose and out through my mouth, until I lull myself back to sleep.

As I'm waiting for drowsiness to overtake me, my mind starts wondering and thinking. If I was dead, then how did I come alive again? Why can't I remember? And most importantly, how did I die? I have a million questions, but no answers. Mother says I'm too young to worry about such things, but it weighs on me, filling my brain with unknowns. I'm only 10 years old, and I don't know a lot of things, but I know something is wrong.

The earliest memories that I have are just snippets of sights and sounds; pictures in my head that don't make any sense. It's the smell of motor oil and cigarette smoke, that I can recall so vividly. It climbed inside my nose and it has stayed there, but I don't know where it came from. It's the vague image of a bottom hem of a summery cotton dress billowing in the breeze, and blood red toe nails encased in brown wedge sandals. It's a huge door slamming shut, the banging that echoes in my head; and the sound of something heavy being dropped on the ground with a loud crash and clank. Mostly though, it is the overwhelming feeling of fear – paralyzing, gut-wrenching, all consuming terror. Then I died.

The mysteries of life continue to prey on my mind, as I live my childhood the best I can. I live in an old farmhouse with my Mother, Rex and Freddie, at the end of an old dirt road, outside a quiet little town in the Heartland. The house, large and in ill repair, and a big wooden barn, sit surrounded by acres of land. There is also a huge wooden garage that sits off to the side. We don't use it anymore. It's gloomy and foreboding, and it scares me. I don't go near it. I don't even walk close to it. Freddie calls me a chicken and dares me to go inside, sometimes taking my arm and trying to drag me over there until I'm screaming and sobbing. Freddie is my brother. He's three years older than me, and he's not scared of the garage. He hides behind it, smoking cigarettes alone, or with his friends. He doesn't think I know, but I know everything. I see everything. But I say little.

Freddie pulls my hair and shoots me with spit balls. We fight a lot, hitting and punching each other until Mother hears us and gets mad, coming after us with a broom that often makes contact with any part of us she can reach. She chases us outside - she doesn't care if we fight out there, as long as she doesn't have to listen. I fend for myself and I fight back. Freddie says he hates me, and I hate him too... most of the time. Sometimes we need to band together – sometimes we need to protect each other – and that is the only time we get along.

Mother and Rex don't believe in sparing the rod and spoiling the child. In fact, they practice the exact opposite. Mother always says sinners needs to be punished. We used to go to church every Sunday. Mother would make us read the Bible while down on our knees in the corner when we misbehaved - or she felt we had - after she had beaten us black and blue, or let any of the successive men in her life discipline us with the belt that used to hang on the wall. It was removed when the local Children's Services visited after school one day - a nice lady who looked over our tidy home and Mother's well behaved children and promptly closed her file and was never seen again. Mother wasn't always religious, but she was excessively so from the time I was 5 until Rex came along. He doesn't believe in God, so now we don't either. But the main thing that stopped Mother going to Church was when she caught wind of some of the parishioners whispering about the mysterious bruises we always seemed to have. We always looked prim and proper - dressed to the nines for Church in our Sunday best - but they could always see a bruise peeking out from under a sleeve, or a discoloured eye that hadn't quite healed by the time Sunday came along. No doubt, because of our visit from the State, we never attended Church again. Mother calls them hypocrites, and continues her form of discipline as she sees fit.

Those church "hypocrites" would be mortified if they knew about the other secret that our family has. I don't even know if I should even mention it, or even think about it. It's a secret so big that we are never allowed to speak of it in my house since it happened...since the whole damn thing happened. I keep my mouth shut, but I remember. We are to pretend none of it ever occurred. We are to ask no questions and never utter a word, lest we get beat black and blue, so I'll just tell you a story. Once upon a time, I had a baby sister, her name was Pearly-May. I think about her often. She was a home birth, born before Rex came along, when it was just Mother, Freddie and myself in the house; in between husbands and steady boyfriends. Mother would be out many nights, always at the bar, often bringing men home who we'd hear coming in, but were always gone in the morning. No one knew who Pearly-May's father was – not even Mother. Freddie and I were waiting by the door, when the doctor came out to tell us we had a sister. We were in awe of the little fingers and toes, as we gazed at her in her crib. But, I think I loved her the most, certainly more than Mother did.

Mother tired of the baby quickly, often leaving her to cry while she sat on the couch watching tv with a drink in her hand, or lying in bed with the curtains drawn all day. She tried for awhile, but she didn't want to be a mother again – she couldn't cope with the demands of a newborn along with two young children who were already an annoyance. I tried to help, but I was too little. Mother was tired and depressed after Pearly-May came. She wanted to go out like she used to, and didn't like being tied down.

Pearly-May didn't last long, just short of a month. Mother says she woke up one morning and found her still and silent in her bassinet. The funny thing is, Mother doesn't realize that I know she's a liar. The baby was not in the bassinet that night. She was in Mother's bed – because I went into that room in the middle of the night when I heard the soft mewling cries. I saw Mother passed out on the bed, an empty bottle of Bourbon on her nightstand. She had laid the baby down on the bed and passed out on top of her. The baby was struggling to breath, to live... I tried with all my might to pull Mother off of her. I tried to pull the baby out from underneath her. I was not strong enough – I was just a baby myself for goodness sake – only three, or maybe four. Freddie slept like the dead himself, so he didn't come when I called for him. I cried and pounded on her, but Mother was dead to the world. The squeaky, breathless cries didn't last long before they stopped. I was terrified, and ran back to my room, jumped in bed and pulled the covers over my head. Shaking and crying, I fell into a sleep of denial – I had dreamed it all, I hadn't seen anything... I never told a soul. Mother was able to tell her story of lies and reap the benefits of sympathy from everyone around her. I never said a word. To this day, I'm pretty sure I imagined the whole thing. Pearly-May died in her sleep, like babies sometimes do, and that's the only truth that I can handle right now. I won't be mentioning Pearly-May again.

II

On a unreasonably warm Saturday morning, I'm sitting up in the big red maple tree in our front yard, high off the ground, leaning against the trunk. One leg swings free, as I pick and bite at my nails, listening to mom and Rex scream at each other from inside the house. Their voices carry loud and angry across the yard. Rex is mother's current husband. He's been around for a couple years so far, and he makes sure to always let me know that he is not my father. He is not Freddie's father either. He is husband number two, and the fourth man who has graced our home since I'm old enough to remember. Rex is a tall, big man, always pulling at his belt to keep his pants from falling down under his large stomach. He yells a lot; he's an angry man. Men come and go. We don't know how long Rex will stay, even if they are married, so Freddie and I don't pay him any mind. We make ourselves scarce; we practically live outside.

I don't remember Mother's first husband, Freddie's father, whose name was Edgar, or maybe it was Edward. I was too young. Mother was 15 when she had Freddie, and was forced to marry his father, as societal rules dictated at the time. It was the proper thing to do, so it was done; no more love involved than that. I was born when Mother and Edgar/Edward were still married, but he wasn't my father. He left when he found out – I was almost two. I think this is why Freddie hates me – he misses his daddy and he blames me for being born and chasing him away. He's never said so, but I know that's what he thinks. I can tell by the look in his eyes. Mother says Freddie's daddy "ran for the hills and never looked back." She giggles when she says this, swirling her ice cubes around in her glass – the glass that is always in her hand. Freddie scowls, but he never says anything. He knows her words are cruel when she has that glass in her hand. After he left, there were several unofficial "fathers", until she married Rex.

Mother tells me over and over again that women need a man to take care of them. She believes that a woman takes care of the house and the husband, and in return, the man takes care of, that is, pays for, the family. She says when I grow up, I have to make sure that I find someone to take care of me. As a result, I have come to believe that I won't be able to take care of myself. Women need men – simple as that – it's been drilled into my head by her words and by her example. Yet, right now, we have no choice but to take care of ourselves, as no one else is taking care of us... not really anyway. Her words are contradictory and confusing, but she must be right. She's an adult after all.

Mother barely provides the necessities, let alone anything extra. She's aloof and unloving, we don't go to her for comfort or hugs. She seems to tolerate us at best. I often catch her looking at both Freddie and I with disdain. It's not a stretch to say we've felt unwanted since we were old enough to realize that she was different than other mothers. She aspires to the air of propriety and perfection to the outside world, but behind closed doors, it's a different matter. But this is the hand I've been dealt and the mother I've been given. Sometimes I wonder why.

Sometimes I grieve for what could have been. Mostly though, I just harden myself and get through every day.

I'm lost in my thoughts until I realize I've bitten my thumb nail down to the quick and it's burning and bleeding a little. I stare at it for a moment, as the screaming rages on inside the house. I tune them out when I see my friend Daisy coming down the road, towards my house. I smile, hopping out of the tree and running up the long driveway to meet her. She lives a few houses up the road and has been my friend since we started school. We met the first day when the boys were teasing her and she was cowering in the corner of the school yard. Daisy's nickname is Upsy – everyone except the teacher calls her that - it's cute and it stuck, but the kids make fun of her. She's shy and quiet, with thick glasses and long pigtails in her hair, which just gives them even more ammunition. Worst of all, she doesn't fight back. So, she needs me.

We meet in the middle of the driveway and I greet her with a big smile and a hug. I love her so much. She's the sister I've chosen for myself, and the person I feel closest to. She's really my only friend in the world, and my safe haven from all the craziness around me. Just her existence makes me happy - she's my distraction, my best friend and my reality. I need to steer her away from the house, so she doesn't hear Mother and Rex yelling. She's heard them fighting before of course, but I don't want her to know that that's all they do. I suggest that we head into the field down by the creek to pick wildflowers. Upsy loves making daisy chains and flower crowns. We skip down the road, and take turns kicking rocks as we go, seeing who can make their rock go the farthest. I could kick harder, but I let Upsy win. It makes her happy.

Down at the creek, we sit cross legged in the tall grass and weave together flowers, wearing our flowery crowns on our heads. We talk in whispers and giggle loudly, sharing secrets and silliness. Mother does not expect me back at any certain time. I never know what time it is. If I miss a meal because I've been gone too long, there won't be another until the next one. Food is pretty scarce anyway, so we just get used to our tummies rumbling and we ignore it. But I can usually sneak a piece of bread when everyone is sleeping, so I'm not anxious to head back to the crazy house.

For a time, Mother tried to keep a garden, to grow us some fresh vegetables in an attempt to save on grocery money. This was quickly abandoned, when she discovered it was hard work, requiring getting out of her daytime dress and getting dirty. She also couldn't bring her glass of booze out there with her, so that was the final straw. She gave up, and the garden withered and died before anything was ever grown and harvested. It is now an overgrown lump in the backyard. Mother does the same with house plants. She ignores them, doesn't tend to them, doesn't water them... and they all die. Our perfectly tidy and pristine house contains several dead plants. It is a metaphor for our lives really – look below the surface, look too hard, and you will see the decay and ugliness underneath, which got there through neglect and lack of care.

We are so involved in what we're doing, that we don't notice the group of boys until they are right close to us. It's Ricky Gartner and his two friends, Billy and Tommy. They are troublemakers, always causing some sort of problem, always sitting in the corner in school. Upsy is startled and shrinks away from their smirks. I roll my eyes and look at them with a sigh.

"What do you want, Ricky Gartner?" I glare at him for interrupting my peace with his inevitable stupidity.

"Nothing Annie Fanny Brewer...." he sneers and looks us over. Billy picks up one of our daisy chains and I snatch it back, before he can break it for no reason.

They are circling us. I pull Upsy to her feet, so we are standing; they won't intimidate us. Upsy stands slightly behind me.

"You best leave us alone!" I warn him.

Tommy snorts and laughs; the three friends grin at each other.

"Or what?" Ricky takes a step closer. I say nothing, but I don't back up. "We're just being friendly. Show them how friendly we are boys." He looks back at his friends.

They lunge at us and start to chase us. We run away, but

Upsy is not fast enough and they catch her easily. She's practically got tears in her eyes, as they shove her back and forth between them. I try to break into their circle to get her away, but they block me.

They are singing, "Upsy Daisy, run around... Upsy Daisy don't make a sound... Upsy Daisy all fall down!" Then they push her to the ground, and stand above her laughing.

I get so mad. They've made her cry. I grab Ricky by the back of the shirt and he turns around to look at me. Before he can react, I punch him square in the nose. I caught him good, because his nose starts to bleed all over his shirt.

He grabs his face and hollers. Tommy and Billy laugh at him, but they don't come after me. They are only his peons, they do what he says, and right now he can't say anything - his eyes are watering from the pain in his nose.

"Annie! I'll get you back! I'll get you back!" he shrieks, trying not sob.

"Get out of here Ricky! Or I'll tell Rex, and he'll come to

your house and pound some sense into you!"

With that, the boys take off running. Everyone in town is scared of Rex, so it's a good threat. Rex probably wouldn't give a care if I told him, but they don't have to know that. In fact, I would never tell him anything.

I help Upsy off the ground and she brushes the dirt off her dress. She has stopped crying, but our fun is over, so we head back towards home.

III

We take the long way back home – going through the woods behind the houses, instead of walking down the road, hoping to avoid those boys. We take our time and walk slowly, we aren't in any rush to get back to our lives at home. Upsy lives with her single mother, and is the middle of 6 children, so she kind of gets lost amongst them. She has as little supervision as I do – people out here live a different life than the city folks. We don't have the worries that the busy cities do. We still leave our doors unlocked and children are expected to stay scarce until dark, with the setting of the sun being our curfew.

The sun is low by the time we make it back to the house. It's silent, there's no more screaming. Mother and Rex are finished fighting, so I invite Upsy inside. As soon as we walk through the door and I close it behind us, I'm met with a shoe that comes flying and hits the wall beside me. I jump, startled – Upsy is wide eyed. Mother comes around the corner screaming. Freddie, who had been sitting on the floor in front of the television, suddenly gets up and runs upstairs; I hear his door slam. He knows what's coming. Upsy flees out the front door. I try to go with her, but a hand grabs me by the scruff of my neck.

Ricky Gartner's mother called her. She knows all about me punching him in the nose. His parents were quite upset. I tried to explain to her what they did to Upsy, why we had to fight back, but she won't let me get a word in edgewise and doesn't care to hear anything I'm saying. Blows reign down upon me, wherever she can reach. All the while, she rants about how I'm an embarrassment to this family, and badly behaved, and can never do anything right. I would never amount to anything, she says over and over again. It's a script really, I hear the same thing every time she's angry. If I can just wait it out, I know it will all be over when the script is over. I try to cover my head as she drags me across the room, yelling and hitting. Rex sits in the reclining chair, smoking a cigar and ignoring everything that's happening around him, focusing only on the football game on the television in front of him. I'm grateful for the fact that he has not been provoked enough to be involved in it this time, because he hits way harder than she does.

She brings me to the foot of the stairs and pushes me forward, yelling at me to stay in my room and I would not be having supper. Falling forward, I bang my knee, and scramble up the stairs to avoid anymore blows. I can hear her downstairs still ranting and raving, then Rex starts yelling back at her to shut up, and another argument ensues. Freddie's bedroom door opens and he sticks his head out. He asks if I'm ok and I nod, wiping my eyes. He shuts his door again. This is the only time I ever see any kindness from him – when one of us is suffering at hands of the adults. We are both bound in the horrors and realities of this house – only then can we relate to each other – otherwise we fight like cats and dogs. I go into my room, prop a chair under the doorknob and fall heavily on the bed. Wiping my eyes, I gingerly touch my sore knee and assess the rest of my injuries. There will be bruises; I always have bruises, but I'll live. This won't kill me. I'm stronger than everything that happens in this house. I survive this existence by being tough, by pretending that none of it fazes me – not the screaming or hitting, or the lack of any real relationship, or love, from anyone in this house. I've developed a tough shell which will protect me for as long as I'm on this earth... most of the time. I'm proud of being a survivor – even if something hurts me, my shell will never crack.

Listening to the yelling downstairs, all I can think about is one thing – the one thing that keeps me going – keeps me from giving up on this depressing existence. When I get old enough...the very moment I get old enough..I'm leaving this place...leaving this house, this town, and this family. I'm getting out of here, faster than a startled jackrabbit. I'm itching to run, crawling out of my skin to get away from this life. I've got big plans to go somewhere exciting and do something important – I'm going to

California, Hollywood specifically, and I'm going to be a model or a movie star. Mother has all sorts of movie magazines laying around and I spend hours pouring over them, studying how to be one of those beautiful women on the pages - how to pose, how to do my hair, how to smile. I'm going to learn whatever I need to learn, so I never need to be here again. I don't tell anyone my plans, not even Upsy. I plan to vanish into thin air – and they can all wonder where I went. They won't ever see me again, because I'm going to leave everything behind me and forget every last one of them. Except Upsy. I expect her to come with me, I just haven't told her that yet. I hold on to these plans deep in my heart and they keep me alive and keep me going in this godforsaken family. I continue to plot my escape as the yelling goes on and on downstairs. As I listen and think, I bite my nails to the quick. The pain of drawing blood distracts me from feeling anything else for awhile.

IV

Someone is standing in my doorway. My room is dark
now, only illuminated by a sliver of moon shining through

my bedroom window. The dark figure puts a hand out towards me, beckoning me to come. I'm not afraid, as I get off the bed and follow. The house is quiet, as we head silently down the stairs and out the front door. I look up at the figure and smile, impossible to discern if it's male or female. I'm happy, wherever we're going. The figure takes my hand, as we step out into the night - a firm grip - and doesn't look down at me. The dew soaked lawn wets the bottom of my feet, as I walk quickly to keep up. Suddenly I realize where we are heading – I'm being brought towards the garage. The imposing and foreboding structure lays in front of us, mere steps away now. I stop walking and dig in my heels, refusing to go any closer. But I'm unable to stand my ground, as I'm being dragged towards the large, wooden door. I try to pull my hand out of the figure's grasp, my feet skidding on the gravel I've been pulled onto. I protest and grunt, and finally I yell. Awaking Mother and Rex is the lesser of two evils right now. I'm struggling and I'm terrified. Crying out in panic, I'm being lead where I do not want to go. The big wooden door swings open, and the blackness summons us in. Pushed blindly into the garage, I hear the door slam shut behind me – then the smell of motor oil and cigarette *smoke fill my nose.....*

I awake with a gasp. Another dream, just another dream... don't scream, don't awaken Mother.... not this time, she's already mad...I force my breathing to slow, my heart beating wildly. Nightmares will follow me the rest of my life... but I'll never confide in anyone, not completely... I'll never reveal my secrets – the ones I know, anyway. There is no one to care.

V

Morning has come and washed away the last vestiges of the night and the terror it brings. There was nothing for breakfast this morning; not enough food in the house again. Mother is too proud and embarrassed to ask for help at the any of the community services. She doesn't want people to know how poor we are. Keeping up airs is very important to her, so we frequently go hungry. I won't have anything to bring to school for lunch either, but I'm not upset. I'm used to it, I convince myself I'm not even hungry anyway. Maybe if I keep not eating, I will get smaller and smaller, and just fade away into oblivion –

maybe oblivion is a better place. Maybe that's where I was when I died all those years ago – I ponder that for a moment, as I get ready for school.

Maybe if I stop in and see Mrs. Delaney on the way home, she'll feed me something. She is our nearest neighbour, a half a mile up the road. 877 steps. Every time I pass by, she's either sweeping her veranda, tending to her flowers, raking the lawn or some such chore. She always waves and then invites me to come and sit with her and drink homemade sweet tea. She's lonely, and will talk on and on, and ask a million questions. Her white hair is always pulled up into a bun with soft tendrils loose around her face. With a kind smile, she always asks me how I'm doing, if I'm hungry, if she can do anything to help... I don't know why she wants to help me, but it feels good to know that somebody is on my side, because when I go home, nobody is ever on my side. She seems to know when I'm hungry. Mother gets mad when she knows I've been taking food from Mrs. Delaney, but a full stomach is worth a smack or two, I figure. Maybe I'll steal a snack from somebody's school bag if I can't make it through the day. The teacher often has fruit on her desk; sometimes I take that too. I've never been caught. I stay quiet as a mouse when she questions the class angrily looking for the thief. And you know what? I don't feel one ounce of guilt. No one has ever made life easy for me, so I do what I need to do to survive. I have a feeling this is the way I am going to be living my life – always doing whatever it takes just to survive. Survival. It's my focus and my goal. I aspire to more, but I barely have what I need to get by. I don't know anything else but fighting to survive.

As I run out the door to meet Upsy to walk to school, I stop on the porch, surprised to see Mother in the yard talking to Uncle Mink, standing beside his big old red convertible. He's sitting at the wheel, with the top down, smoking a cigarette. He's wearing a brown straw fedora with a black band around it, and a smirk on his face. They both turn and notice me when the door slams.

"Uncle Mink offered to drive you to school this morning." Mother looks over her horn-rimmed glasses at me.

"No thank you. I'm meeting Upsy to walk with her." I reply. "Same as every day." I add under my breath.

"Aw come on Sweet Pea," he groans exaggeratedly loud, "you're breaking my heart. Hop in here with Unc." He gestures to the seat beside him, cigarette hanging out his mouth while he talks.

Byron Minkus has never been called by his real name his entire life. Everyone knows him only as Mink; he is Mother's brother. They share a mother, whose family lives on the Eastern seaboard, whom they both couldn't wait to get away from. I feel that. He used to come over a lot when I was younger. He even babysat Freddie and I for a spell when Mother got a job at the local bar – which lasted only until she was caught stealing money from the tip jar. I don't remember Mother working, or being babysat, but I was young. I only know what I was told. Uncle Mink doesn't come over hardly at all anymore since then.

A long time ago, he was in the Army, had gotten hurt and received an honorable discharge. He walks with a limp and a cane, and as a result takes a lot of pain medication, which he liberally mixes with whatever booze he drinks all day. I'm not sure he even ever saw any real combat, but he likes to tell stories about the people he supposedly killed. I never pay any attention to his tales of blood and gore. He's trying to be scary and intimidating, but he's just posturing; it doesn't scare me. He's been in and out of jail for the last several years and lives a rather nomadic life, having had no real fixed address for quite awhile. Occasionally he shows up unexpectedly.... and unwanted, as far as I'm concerned. He gives me a bad feeling, and I have learned to listen to my bad feelings.

I'm eyeballing him with a slight sneer on my lips, contemplating running right past them both, into the woods and taking the back way to school to avoid going to school with him, when Upsy comes up the driveway, book bag in hand.

"Sorry, there's Upsy. Gotta go." I bound down the steps and as I'm running past the car, he reaches out and grabs my arm. I yank it away and glare at him.

"I can drive you both you know. There's lots of room." He curls his lip into a half smile.

Mother tells me not to be rude and get in the car. Upsy is excited about riding in a convertible, so I relent.

"Your friend can ride up here with me in the front. You can sit in the back, sour puss." he says.

Upsy happily jumps in the front seat and I begrudgingly get in the back and sit with my arms folded across my chest.

"Bye Louise," he calls to Mother with a salute, as he starts the car and peels out in a cloud of dust.

Uncle Mink is talking to Upsy, but I can't make out anything that's being said because of the noise of the wind in my ears and rumble of the motor. Upsy is laughing and Mink is grinning at her. He looks into the back at me and says something – Upsy giggles again. They are both annoying me and I can't wait to get out of this car.

He stops at the gas station, turning the engine off.

"Be a good girl Annie and go get me a pack of the smokes

- red box, same as this here." He shows me his empty pack and tosses me a few bills.

"We need to get to school..." I start protesting but he cuts me off.

"Be a good girl..." he snarls, emphasizing "good". A shiver runs up my spine, for a reason I can't explain. I take his money and go into the store.

No one pays me any mind, as I go over to the big cigarette machine in the corner, chose the right box and pull the long handle to release the box of poison into the tray below. As I retrieve it, I look up at the magazine rack beside me. Sticking the cigarette package in my pocket, I pull out a movie magazine. Opening it up, I thumb through the pages, looking at the beautiful women and handsome men – Hollywood stars, rich and famous, and don't know how lucky they are. Little girls like me are desperately wanting, even needing, to live the life they take for granted. Blondes and brunettes pose with pursed lips in fancy dresses, ample cleavage visible. I purse my lips too, and I study... and practice.... I'm going to be one of them one day, so I need to learn how to achieve the very thing that will get me out of this town. It's not optional, this has to happen, this needs to happen.... I need to make it happen. I look around, still no one is paying any attention to me at all. I slip the magazine under my shirt, pull the cigarettes out of my pocket and walk out of the store. No hesitation, no guilty face, just like a pro....just like so many times before. No one ever buys me anything, there's not enough money for gifts in my family – often not enough money for necessities, so I take what I want. No one looks out for me, does for me... so I do for myself.

I go back to the car, get in the back and toss the cigarettes into the front seat. Uncle Mink looks back at me and nods, starting the car. It takes me a moment to realize that both of them in the front seat are now quiet – no more talking and laughing. Uncle Mink is concentrating on driving. Upsy is looking out the side window, silent. I reach between the seat and the door and poke her arm. She doesn't respond, she just keeps looking out the window. I shrug and take out my magazine so I can keep practicing.

At the school, Upsy jumps out of the car as soon as it stops and runs into the little white building. I don't say thank you, but I do look at Uncle Mink and say, "We walk to school – don't pick us up again." He gives a laugh, tipping his hat as I get out and slam the door behind me. His car kicks up dirt and pebbles spray my legs as he drives away.

VI

Upsy is quiet most of the day, but by afternoon break, she's pretty much back to normal. Everyone is allowed to be moody sometimes, so I don't ask her about it. We walk around the schoolyard, talking in hushed tones about stuff only we care about. Ricky and the boys move out of the way when they see us coming. I don't think they'll bother us again; it was worth incurring Mother's wrath. You have to show people how to treat you. You can't let them walk all over you. I might have to put up with hurt at home, but I do not have to put up with it at school. It's important to be tough in this life. I don't have a lot of friends besides Upsy, because I think a lot of the kids are scared of me. But I'd rather them be afraid, than me be weak, be a doormat. At home, I have to bottle up all my feelings to save myself, but at school, I can be whoever I want. I have a lot of anger festering in me, and sometimes, it comes out whether I want it to or not.

I find school pretty boring actually. I'm not dumb, but I'm not interested in taking tests, reading things that don't interest me, doing math, working on projects – none of it suits me at all. I spend a lot of time biting on my pencil and looking out the window, daydreaming of a life that could be mine, will be mine. My grades aren't great, but I keep passing from grade to grade...barely. Mother has finally given up trying to beat smart into me when I bring home a bad mark, so I just put in my time until it's time for me to leave – this school, this town, this life. Upsy, on the other hand, loves school. She gets to get away from her house full of siblings, where nobody pays much attention to her. Upsy is what they call "teacher's pet", so she basks in the teacher's attention. Mrs. Wembley has taken a shine to her and Upsy soaks in everything she doesn't get at home. Her mother loves her of course, never hits her, she just has too many children. Upsy especially likes the fact that Mrs. Wembley only calls her Daisy, never using her nickname. The rest of us are just used to calling her Upsy, which was given to her by some relative of hers when she was born. Nobody can remember who. She tells me sometimes she doesn't like that nickname anymore, but it continues to stick.

Walking home from school is always the last moment of peace in my day. I'm always anxious, even trepidatious on the walk home, because I never know what I'm going to be walking into when I get there. By that time of the day, Mother always has her glass full of ice cubes and liquor in her hand – she's usually had a couple by then, and usually continues with a few more until bedtime. Her drink of choice is bourbon from a fancy bottle in the liquor cabinet. The cabinet is never locked – it's used too frequently to bother. Once, when I was home alone, I got the bottle out and twisted the top off, examining the smooth brown liquid inside. When I sniffed it, it gave me a jolt – it was enough to clear my nose out. It smelled worse than the cans of varnish in the basement. I didn't know how anyone would want to drink that, but I dared myself to try. When I hesitated, I double dared myself, so then I had to of course. I closed my eyes and threw the bottle back, taking a large mouthful and swallowing it down. It was like drinking gasoline! I coughed and choked and sputtered. My mouth and throat burned and the inside of my chest got so warm, I thought I was on fire and burning up from the inside out. I was sure I was dying. Mother was going to come home and find me dead on the floor with the bottle of bourbon beside me. That would serve her right. But I recovered. For a long time, I would wonder what the fascination was with drinking that poisonous swill – every adult I was around drank their poison of choice. At the time I didn't realize that the roots of addiction had already taken hold deep within me, no thanks to hereditary and genes. Unfortunately, I would forget that traumatizing experience and let the shadow of dependency get hold of me also. It was to become another tool I would develop and latch onto to cope and survive. But I get ahead of myself...

<u>Years of Sorrow</u>

I

The school year is over and the endless days of summer

stretch before us. Upsy and I spend countless days wandering around aimlessly, taking long walks down the dirt road between our houses and beyond. We swim in the creek, laying on the riverbank afterwards finding shapes in the clouds. Playing make believe in the woods, where the trees are our kingdom, we climb as high as we dare, before chickening out and climbing back down. We eat suppers of wild raspberries and blueberries, or sometimes Upsy might bring us sandwiches her mother makes, so we'll have a picnic in the tall grass. We never run out of things to do. Mother doesn't care where I am during the day, as long as I'm home by dark.

On July 4th, Upsy and I celebrate my birthday. I'm a Independence Day baby, which means my birthday is a day of celebration for everyone, every year. How ironic it is to be born on a day that represents freedom and peace, when my life is anything but free and peaceful. Upsy and I watch the Town fireworks down by the water, and mark the occasion by sharing a chocolate bar that I stole from the store earlier that day when no one was looking. It will be the only acknowledgement that I was born, that I exist, other than Mother muttering Happy Birthday, as she poured herself a drink.

Upsy and I often walk into town and window shop, staring longingly at the fancy clothes and jewellery in the shop windows, or even the delicious looking treats in the bakery. If we're lucky, the bakery owner will give us a small treat that isn't perfect enough to sell to the rich people who frequent the shop. If we are unlucky, we root through the garbage bin out back, sometimes finding the sweetest treasures. The well dressed men and women in town often look down their noses at us. It's a small town, and everyone knows we are the country folk who live on the outskirts. If they don't already know Rex, whose reputation precedes him thanks to his constant bar brawling and police involvement, or they don't know Upsy's mother Mary, who is the woman with a million kids, then our clothes and unkempt appearance are certainly dead giveaways. My long blonde hair is always unruly, unless Mother gets a hold of me and roughly runs a brush through it. I dress like a tomboy in ripped up jeans and t shirts. Upsy always wears pigtails, but her hand-me-down dresses are often a bit too big, too small, or sometimes stained. Mrs. Delaney never looks down on us, she just calls us rag-a-muffins with a small smile on her face.

I haven't visited Mrs. Delaney in awhile and we are so thirsty, so on the way home from town on a sweltering afternoon in July, we found ourselves walking up the long dirt driveway to her large white clapboard home with the wraparound porch. She had lived there by herself since her husband Elmer died five years ago. I remember Elmer as a large man, who always with a smile on his face, just like his wife. He was a farmer his whole life, but at the end, he had to let the livestock and crops go due to his failing health and inability to work the farm. He kept the chickens though, and worked a large egg production, selling to the neighbouring towns. When he died, he left a little nest egg for his wife. Mrs. Delaney always laughs when she tells people that – her nest egg came from selling eggs – she thinks that's so funny. She still keeps some chickens and carries on selling, but it's becoming increasingly more difficult for her by herself.

The chickens are squawking and clucking, running around freely in the yard, as she opens the doors to greet us as we reach the porch. Upsy chases one up the driveway and I laugh at her. She chases those chickens around the yard with delight every time. Mrs. Delaney especially enjoys watching her, getting a chuckle watching Upsy scurry around the yard, not unlike the chickens themselves.

"Well hello girls, I'm glad you're here to visit... was getting a might lonely. I'd tell you to come in the house, but it's 150 degrees in there, we best sit on the porch." She smiles, as we sit on the wicker furniture and she sits on the creaky rocking chair beside us. She's brought out a pitcher of homemade lemonade, with lemons floating around inside.

We are so thirsty that Upsy and I down the first glass all at once. Mrs. Delaney laughs and fills us up again. I wipe the sweat off my forehead, while she asks us how our mothers are. I know she asks, not to be nosy, but out of concern for us. She knows our families are poor, Upsy is pretty much neglected, but not purposely so. She also knows that Mother and Rex drink a lot. She sees the police cars racing to our house once in a while when they fight a bit too hard. She hears the yelling and the screaming, when she walks by our house on her daily walks. And she sees the bruises that are often easily visible on Freddie and me, and even on Mother sometimes.

Mrs. Delaney has known Mother for years, watched her grow up and have a family of her own. She's seen Mother with boyfriend after boyfriend, and already on her second husband in her 20's. She also knows Uncle Mink, and she doesn't like him either. She says he makes the hair on the back of her neck stand up, but she doesn't tell me why. She knows our history; she knows more than I do. She doesn't want to get involved and get Mother in trouble, but she keeps her eye on things, just in case.

"How are those nightmares of yours, Annie?" Mrs. Delaney asks, blotting her sweaty face with a handkerchief. The air is humid and the slight breeze isn't enough to cool us down.

Besides Upsy, Mrs. Delaney is the only one I've confided in about my dreams. I don't go into too much detail about the horror they contain, because even in the light of day, it is too scary to say the words out loud. Oh, Mother knows I have dreams of course, but she doesn't know what they're about – she's never asked. I wouldn't have told her anyway. But sometimes, they scare me so much, that I've told Mrs. Delaney, hoping she can help me make sense of them. She really can't, but it makes me feel better to talk about it and get it out of my head.

"I'm still having 'em. Sometimes worse than others, sometimes I wake up before they get to far. Other times, I can't wake up at all." I reply, pulling my long hair up off the nape of my neck and running an ice cube out of my glass over my neck and face to cool down. A trickle of melting ice runs down the back of my shirt.

Mrs. Delaney sighs, and says firmly, "Well I'm sure one day, you are going to outgrow those old bad dreams. One day they are just going to fade away, and you'll forget they ever existed. Or maybe you'll figure out what's causing them and be able to get rid of them once and for all." She looks thoughtful for a moment, then adds, "If I was a superstitious sort, I'd say maybe those awful dreams are harbingers of bad things to come, bad omens of sorts...."

she dismisses this thought with a flick of hand, "but I'm not superstitious one bit, so pay no mind to what I just said."

I shrug, trying to disregard her words. But the seed was planted. Could she be right? Are my bad dreams a foreshadowing? Do I have "the gift"? Mother once spoke of a great aunt of hers having "the gift". Now I'm trying to remember if anything bad happens after I have a nightmare. I don't think so, but it's hard to tell because so many bad things happen in my world. I wouldn't know the difference really. I'm sure she's wrong. I can't predict anything; my bad dreams mean nothing. I think they are just going to be with me until I'm old enough to get away from the house and the people who are causing them. When I leave this town, my mind will be free and the dreams will stop. I just have to hold on awhile longer. I can do that. My days are often hellish and difficult, so I look forward to the time when I can have peaceful nights - a few hours of escape instead of the madness of the day following me into my sleep.

Upsy sits quietly, sipping her drink and watching the

chickens. She's not a great conversationalist. No one at home talks to her much, or asks her what she thinks about things, so she's never learned to be outspoken or social. She's shy, so she needs me.

II

An overnight thunderstorm begins, bringing with it much needed rain. Lightening flashes, illuminating the sky, and thunder crashes – a cacophony of noise wakes me. I'm disoriented and sleepy, it's so loud. I struggle to open my eyes, fighting with sleep to let me wake up. It's dark, it's cold, there's a bad odour. There's something hard underneath me. I prop myself up on my elbows, trying to see. Another lightening flash, followed quickly by a large boom – my eyes adjust briefly then it goes dark again – something is wrong. Flash, boom – I bolt upright. I'm in the garage! Why am I sleeping in the garage?! How did I get here? My heart starts racing. Flash of light, crash of thunder, so loud the earth seems to shake around me. The storm is right overhead; the lightening flickering as though electricity is going off and on, off and on. Only then do I see the dark figure standing in the corner. I can't scream, my mouth is frozen open, but nothing comes out. It starts to move, walking towards me slowly with it's hand held out. I want to run but I can't. Then the smell of motor oil and cigarettes fills my nose. The figure moves closer. I withdraw as far away from it as I can, shrinking backwards on the cold cement floor, until my head hits something. I look up and above me there's second dark figure looking down at me, almost faceless, save for bright red lips curled into a clownish smile. That's when I scream......

What does it all mean?

III

Holidays and birthdays have usually passed without much acknowledgement in my world. They cost money, which we don't have, so Mother would just as soon act like they are just regular days. We learned a long time ago not to whine or complain, but we are well aware that we are going without while everyone else is celebrating. But, there is one holiday that even us poor children can enjoy. Halloween. It is the best time of the year, as far as I'm concerned. It doesn't cost any money – we create our own costumes from whatever we can find around the house. Mother doesn't care what we do as long as we don't mention money.

When Mother first married Rex, he worked in town at a garage as a mechanic and there was finally income coming into the house after a long stretch of scraping by with what Mother got from the State. However, he quickly lost his job shortly after they were married. Mother told us, and everyone else, that he had been laid off, but it was well known that he had been fired. Too much boozing resulted in him being frequently late, going home early, or being too hungover to go in at all. Then, when he went to work one morning still drunk from the night before, his boss had had enough. Rex blamed being fired on Mother, telling her she was a bad influence on him because of her drinking problem. Those may have been the only true words he ever spoke. That was a bad fight; police were called – Freddie and I cowered in the pantry listening to the screams and punches being thrown. We were never too scared for Mother though – she always gave as good as she got. When the police left, after finding us in our hiding spot, and before they sent us to bed because this was "adult business" they said, we saw both Mother and Rex with bloody noses – Rex with a gash on his forehead from a pot Mother had wielded. The last thing we heard, while we were still quaking from fear, was the police chuckling to each other quietly as they left, that "these two country wackos really deserved each other". The police continued to come out every time they were called on Mother and Rex, or Mother and any of her other men, but Freddie and I soon realized that we were alone in this game – no one was going to save us.

No one else would hire Rex after he was fired by one of the most reputable employers in town, due to his reputation as an unreliable worker, a heavy drinker, and a brawler. He settled into a slump of sitting on the couch with a beer in his hand all day. He gained weight, got bigger and meaner. For a time, he tried fixing people's cars in our old garage for cash. The long-unused building came alive for a time, so Rex could eke out a minuscule living. I refused to go near it, resulting in some good whoopings when Rex wanted me to fetch him a beer, or some other reason which would have resulted in me having to go in there. I deliberately disobeyed, and that would make him some mad, but I stood my ground and took my lumps - it was preferable than going near that place. So, Rex provided some income, until one day, a jack let go and a car fell on his leg. Now he walks with a limp and, on bad days, a cane, just like Uncle Mink. When he could no longer fix vehicles, as he no longer had the physical ability to stand for very long, or get up and down and move around the vehicle because of his leg, the old garage was closed up for the final time. Since then, it sits as it is. As it was. A large entity with a life of its own that seemingly haunts my dreams.

I'm 11 now, and this Halloween begins as every other one does. Since it falls on a weekend, Upsy and I are able to spend the day making our costumes. We go to her house and root through trunks and boxes in her attic until we find just what we needed. Upsy finds a headband, makes two ears out of felt and finds a black leotard to wear under a black bathing suit and, just like that, she's a cat – painting whiskers on her face to complete the look. This year I'm going to dress like a movie star, one of the glamour girls in the movie magazines. Halloween is the one night of the year that I can pretend to be anything, anyone I want – and believe me, anyone else is preferable to being Annie Brewer.

I find just what I'm looking for in an old box in the back corner of the Upsy's attic. A glamorous old ball gown that had been packed away for years. It is made of red satin, flowing and long, with a v-neck, spaghetti straps and a tight bodice. It is the most beautiful thing I've ever seen, and looks exactly like something a movie star would wear – I fall in love with it instantly. With no one's permission, I take scissors to it and cut it down, so I won't be tripping over the length. When Upsy accidentally rips it, I have to cut it a bit higher than I want, but am still satisfied that it sits above knee length. Putting it on, I feel beautiful. Looking in the mirror, I gasped at how it changed me, made me look older, sophisticated...like a real person, like someone who deserves all the good things in life. A far cry from from the pathetic way I usually exist in life. We find a long, wavy brown wig in another box, and a pair of red high heels, which although they are too big, I will wear proudly, despite the risk of breaking an ankle. It's a risk I'm willing to take to feel like a movie star, if only for one night. Upsy sneaks some of her mother's make up and paints my lips a garish red. We ooh and ahh at ourselves in the mirror, taking one last look before we grab our pillow cases and head out the door, with Upsy's mother too busy with the younger children and the baby to pay us any mind.

We decide we'll walk into town and then catch the houses on our road on the way back home. It's twilight, with the sun starting to sink low in the sky. We walk in the direction of the pink and yellow sunset, looking forward to just being children for awhile. It's chilly and I regret not bringing a sweater or a shawl, but I don't want to cover my beautiful costume, so I brave the cold. I walk most of the way carrying the high heeled shoes, as they are impossible to walk in on the dirt road. When we get to town, we follow a trail of kids going door to door. We get some odd looks at some houses, people taking a moment to pause and just stare. Maybe it's because I'm a little bit stumble-y in the shoes. I pay them no mind; we're used to being stared at by the town folk. A gang of boys follow us down the street for awhile, making fun and calling us names – I don't understand the words, the names they are calling, but they stop when I put my bag of candy down and throw rocks at them.

After filling our bags as full as we can, we make our way
back home, down the long dirt road from town to country.
It is proper dark now, a bright full moon leading us home.
As we walk we eat our candy, leaving a trail of wrappers
behind us. We part at Upsy's house, and she runs happily
up her driveway to show her mother her bag of loot. I
want to stop at Mrs. Delaney's, whose house I pass next,
and show her my beautiful dress, maybe even share my
dream of getting out of this hick town and going to
Hollywood to become a star, but her lights are all off, so I
don't bother. I continue on home, where the lights are all
on, outside and in.

I approach warily, something warning me to turn and run
the other way, but I'm cold; I need to go in. Before I can
reach the porch, Mother opens the door; she'd seen me
coming, and had been pacing a groove in the floor waiting
for me to appear. She storms off the steps and bounds over
to me, grabbing me roughly by the arm. She looks down at
me with a storm of anger on her face. Her brows are
deeply furrowed and her eyes are glazed with rage.

Someone from town had called her. Someone told her that her daughter was walking around wearing something of a "questionable nature" for a costume.

"What on earth are you wearing?! How dare you walk around town looking like a tramp – a cheap, two bit hooker – that's what you look like! A common whore!" She screams in my face. That's the words the boys had been saying too. I don't know what those words mean. I don't know what's wrong. In my mind, I am beautiful. I am a movie star. I am somebody. Mother drags me screaming and crying into the house and up the stairs, all the while shouting how I am bringing shame upon the family and my costume is likely all I'll amount to in life anyway...good for nothing...pain in the ass...blah blah blah...it goes on and on for an eternity. By the end of the beating, the beautiful dress has been ripped off me, and ends up in a pile of tatters and rags. My lipstick is smeared all over my face, mixed with my tears. Mother threw out my candy. And now I know what those words mean.

IV

I'm not the only one living a life of hell. Freddie has his
own battles to fight. Rex mostly ignores me, but he is
always hard on Freddie. I watch my brother being given
impossible tasks to complete, being set up to fail, and then
getting the daylights beat out of him when he does. It's like
a game Rex plays with Freddie. When Rex has been
drinking, it's even worse. Freddie tries to stay away from
the house, but eventually he has to come home, eventually
Rex finds him. Often, for no reason, he will walk by
Freddie and cuff him upside the head, or give him a shove
as Freddie walks past. Once he shoved him while he had
his dinner plate in his hand, making him drop the plate and
sending his food all over the floor. Freddie was made to sit
and eat off the floor, then clean up the broken plate.
There's no point in complaining to Mother, she's present
for most of it and just looks the other way.

Freddie feels as hopeless and defeated as I do, a burning
rage grows and festers in him, same as the one that
smoulders deep in my own heart. He often takes his
frustrations out on me, for lack of anywhere else to vent. I
know that all the fighting and other mean things he does to
me is just displaced rage meant for Rex...and likely

Mother. I understand, but it still hurts. One minute he hates me and the next minute he's my friend; the only other person who understands what it's like to live in Louise Brewer's world. I know he can't get wait to get away from here, from her, either. He also can't wait to get away from me - because I represent our stilted and sad childhood - and he doesn't want to see me anymore than he wants to see anyone else in this life we haven't chosen. He's older than me, so I know he's going to take off one day and leave me alone here. That thought terrifies me.

It happened on a bright, sunny day in late Spring when I was almost 12. I had to stay after school, for pinching a girl who pulled Upsy's hair. Coming home, the house is eerily quiet. Rex's old truck is still parked in the yard, so someone must be around. I tip-toe quietly through the house, unsure of what's happening. The living room is empty and still. I head into the kitchen and out the back door. Freddie is sitting on the back steps under the clothesline, his knees folded up to his chest and his head bent down on them. His back is heaving with silent sobs. I sit beside him, saying nothing. He looks up at me with a tear-stained face and a bloody lip; a bruise forming on his cheek.

"What's wrong?" I ask quietly, afraid to hear the answer.

"Rex accused me of stealing the five dollars in his wallet. I ain't never touched it!" he says earnestly, and I know he's telling the truth.

"Where is he?" I ask, and before he can answer, the back door is ripped open and there stands Rex in a drunk-fuelled rage – face red and sweaty, breathing heavy.

Freddie jumps up and off the back steps and backs away shaking his head. I jump off the steps too and try to stay hidden beside them.

"You little no good liar, you better give me that five dollar bill you stole. I done told you!" Rex sounds like a monster.

"I didn't take it!" Freddie pleads, he's desperate now. He looks around, wanting to run away, but he knows it will be even worse when Rex finds him – Rex always finds him.

"Then if you don't have it, who took it?! Huh boy? You better spill it now or you'll be sorry." Rex is coming down the stairs heading towards Freddie. I cover my eyes and peak through my fingers, unable to move, but unable to look away.

Freddie is looking all over nervously, trying to figure out what to do. Rex is coming closer and closer, shouting and threatening, demanding to know where his money is.

Freddie, in his desperation, locks eyes on me. Oh no...no...

"Annie took it!" He shouts, pointing at me. I'd like to believe that he did so without thinking, a reckless statement that now makes me the object of Rex's drunken fury.

He turns on me and starts lumbering forwards with a limping shuffle.

I shriek and take off running, seeing Freddie sink to the ground on his knees in relief.

I can easily outrun Rex, but I need to find a place to hide -
until Rex passes out drunk, or drinks enough to forget. I
don't know where to go. The yard and woods behind are
wide open, offering no cover. I run towards the barn,
hoping Rex doesn't see me dart in there. Once inside, I
search frantically for a hiding spot. The old horse paddocks
and piles of loose hay and hay bales aren't good enough.
The only thing I can think to do is run up the old rickety
ladder to the loft above and hope Rex can't get up there.

He enters the barn, the effort of coming after me showing
in his face, as he spits and wheezes and spots me up in the
loft. I shake my head and back away as he's coming up the
ladder. Surely it can't hold his weight. He's drunk and
slow, but sure enough, he's making his way up. A final
grunt puts him at the top, and he's walking towards me still
shouting about his money.

I feel cornered and frightened. I'm mute, and can only
shake my head and keep backing away. My heart is
pounding wildly in my chest, a fight or flight response
setting in. Rex isn't sure-footed as he approaches me, so
that's why I don't know what exactly happens next. Did he

stumble and fall, or did I reach out and push him in an effort to keep him away from me? I'll never know, I'll never be sure.

What did happen was Rex fell off the top of the loft and landed in the tall haystack below. In the haystack was a pitchfork that had been hiding there for years, since the last time anyone had the need to fork hay. Someone had set it upright against a load-bearing post and hay was piled around it, leaving it stuck out just enough... Farmers know never to do that...most humans with common sense know not to do that...but done was done, and it had sat like that for many years. Rex had impaled himself on the old rusty tines, and died with his eyes wide open in shock. The hay surrounding him quickly turned crimson with his blood.

We found out later that Mother had taken his precious five dollars to go to town and buy herself a bottle of cheap booze.

Freddie and I never told anyone what happened. He was found by Mother hours later when she returned home. We were in the house, in our rooms waiting for the inevitable screaming. She did not disappoint.

V

With Rex gone, Mother sank into a deep depression. There
was a long stretch of time where she took to her bed and
wouldn't leave her room, except to to come out and re-fill
her liquor glass. She lay there day after day, with the
curtains drawn in the blackness and silence. She was
mourning in her own way, I suppose, but she was also
trying to figure out how she was going to survive now.
Mother had no idea how to exist without a man. She
couldn't be alone – she just didn't know how. She wasn't a
complete person. She had taught me, by example, that I
wasn't either. Little did I know I would grow up to follow
in her footsteps, but again, I get ahead of myself.

Nice neighbours had provided us with food and
expressions of sympathy at first, but eventually the visits
stopped. They were sorry, but not too sorry – Mother didn't
have many friends and Rex was not well liked. Mrs.
Delaney offered her condolences as sincerely as she could,
but her dislike for Rex was well known. She later told me

in private that we were better off without him.

Freddie and I didn't mourn, we didn't feel guilty, we didn't feel anything. We just waited. I didn't blame Freddie for pointing the blame at me, and he didn't question what happened in that barn. Eventually mother showed her true colours, and surprised us with her ability to flip her emotions off and on like a switch. Just like that, several weeks later, she had decided she had mourned enough.

She started getting dressed again, all dolled up in a face full of makeup and donning her best costume jewellery. She started going into town again and nodding politely at the townsfolk, even though every single one of them looked down their noses at her. She wore her fancy hats and high heeled shoes to do simple errands. She thought she was fitting in with the regular people, the "normal" people. She wanted to be seen as their equal, command their respect – she was a lady in mourning after all. But after all her prim and proper masquerading during the day, at night she turned back into the person she was before she married Rex.

VI

Months have passed since Rex's death. Mother has removed all evidence of him from the house. All his clothes, pictures, personal affects, were all sold or given away, and whatever was left was burned in a fire pit in the backyard. It was like he never existed, and that was fine with Freddie and I. It made it easier to forget, and we have succeeded in burying the memory of his demise way deep down until the details are murky and muddled and we can almost believe that we aren't aware of what actually happened. Almost.

I'm 13 now. I'm growing up, growing out and getting taller. Boys are starting to look at me funny... as are some of the more questionable men in town. Their leering looks and cat calls make me uncomfortable. At first, I wear layers of shirts and cover every inch of skin so they have nothing to look at. I hadn't worn a dress since that Halloween night. Mother warns me against boys and their evil intentions and threatens me with all sorts of horrors if I ever return their attentions. But out of the other side of her mouth, she keeps telling me, and showing me, that it's necessary to have a man to take care of me. Her mixed messages are confusing.

Mother proves herself to be the utmost hypocrite, as she continually brings around man after man trying to fill the void Rex left. Many nights, and often for days at a time, she will leave Freddie and I alone while she searches for a new man, a new husband, a new father for her children - for someone to take care of her, and to provide for her family. She's terrified of poverty, even though it's been her lifestyle certainly for my entire life, and likely as long as she can remember. She knows it can get worse, and after hearing her on the phone one day, I know that she's afraid of losing the house. She had inherited it from her grandmother, and had lived in it most of her life, because her grandmother practically raised her, according to her. She's having a hard time even scraping up enough money to keep the bank happy since Rex died. His small insurance policy has kept us going this far, but it's fast running out, in part due to the amount being spent on her beloved bourbon. It never even strikes her that maybe she could get a job and take care of herself – she's floundering around helplessly and refusing to grasp at the most obvious lifeline. I watch Mother carefully, without even wanting to, meaning to...I'm at a vulnerable, impressionable age...I'm learning all the wrong things. She's my only role model. Even though I will still cling to my dreams of being a movie star, I too, subconsciously, will grow up searching for someone to take care of me. But, really, I was just trying to find someone to love me, to show me love, in whatever form I could get it.

The amount of stress she's under makes Mother even more angry and cruel, devoid of any patience or caring. She's quick to lash out with a slap to the face, or a belt to wherever she can make contact with. She and Freddie have frequent battles, as he is getting older and become more rebellious and out of control. He begins hanging around with a group of bad boys, committing minor crimes; theft and vandalism. He quickly gets a criminal record – but I know that's not who he is. He's just damaged, hurting, and he's taking all his rage out around him and on himself. As I get older, I understand more and more. The little boy who used to terrorize me and fight with me isn't actually a bad guy. He's actually a good kid – internalizing the pain around him. He's found a place to fit in and is doing whatever it takes to be accepted by that group. He just wants to be whole, as do the rest of us. He hangs around the house less and less. There's no one around to protect me anymore.

Most of the men Mother brings by are harmless, albeit not the most upstanding citizens. We meet some - the ones who hang around for awhile, who pass through our house, some just spending a night, some living with us for weeks or even months. The others, we only hear about, as she regales us with stories. Mother entertains them all with a personality that we, her children, have never seen before. She's animated and cordial, polite and friendly. There's a fake-ness about her – we know she's putting it on, being who she's really not – in an attempt to attract and keep someone, anyone. Her fear of being alone makes her reek of desperation.

It is when she brings home Cleve Braithwaite, that I discover the disconnect between men and women, the power women can wield over men, and the complex relationships between the two. It also firmly cements in my mind the notion that men are not to be trusted; their ulterior motives are always lurking below the surface. In my limited life experience, I have come to believe that all men are the same really, I've never come across one that was worth a spit. I never had a male role model to show me that some men could be loving and kind, have integrity or be trustworthy. I've never had a kindly old grandfather to spoil me, or a father of my own to call me his princess. I've only been privy to the numerous men that mother has paraded through our lives, and Uncle Mink – who practically lives in the metaphorical gutter of society.

Cleve is a bit younger than Mother, but this is likely through no fault of his own. He probably doesn't even know her real age, since she dolled herself up to the point where one couldn't really be sure. He's a tall, thin man, with hair a bit too long and a thin moustache, who met Mother at the bar - the one she frequents - the same one where he plays guitar with the local house band at night. During the day, he's a blue collar worker, which seems to be the only type that will give her the time of day. Mother has never been successful at attracting a man who wears a suit to work every day. She would be in her glory if she ever did. Cleve likes to call himself a business owner, self employed, but in reality, he's a glorified handyman, keeping himself afloat with cash jobs of menial labour, and the few dollars he makes playing guitar at night. Like her other men, he liked his booze as well, and we never saw him without a drink in his hand. He wasn't a mean drunk, so that was a small thing to be thankful for.

When I first meet Cleve, he shakes my hand proper, but I notice right away the sly side eye he gives me all the time. His exaggerated friendliness and over attentiveness also seems to bother Mother. She makes sure we are never in the same room together alone. I'm thankful for this, as I thought she was protecting me, but I soon come to realize that she's jealous of the attention he's paying me. She starts treating me like competition for this man's attention. Whenever he tries to talk to me, she interrupts and draws him away, which I'm happy for. But I know this is driving a bigger wedge in between us. I can't help the fact that I'm getting older, I can't stop the passage of time, in fact I would hurry it along if I could. This new development makes being in this house, being around her, even more uncomfortable. Is this the way that men treat women - like they are merely something to be harassed and bothered and flirted with? Is this one of the secrets of growing up and being an adult? Something to be tolerated – the price you pay in order to be taken care of? And is this the way a mother treats a daughter? To see her as competition for a man who is no prize? I don't know how to convince her that I'm not her rival.

Cleve has lived in our house for a couple of months now. I've been successful at avoiding him for the most part. I make sure that my door is locked at night, just in case. I make sure that I'm fully dressed at all times, never caught coming out of the bathroom in a towel. I don't engage him in any conversation and even avoid looking at him or making eye contact. I feel uncomfortable in my own house, in my own skin. I hate being a girl right now – I hate my very being. I avoid the house as much as I can. Still, despite my precautions, he's constantly trying to talk to me, finding reasons to touch me – a hand on the shoulder, a pat on the back. It makes Mother bristle every time. I feel the chasm between us becoming wider and wider.

I'm sitting on the couch flipping through a magazine one

evening, when he comes and sits down beside me, wrapping his arm around my shoulder and pretending to be interested in what I'm looking at. I squirm a bit and pull away to the side, trying to put a bit of distance between us. He's close enough that I can smell him; a mix of cheap cologne and beer, as he breathes on me, trying to make small talk. He's telling me which of the movie actresses he thinks are pretty and why, that I look like the pretty blonde ingenue on page 12, that I'd sure look pretty in that dress.... Glancing up at Mother, I see her keeping an eye on us, as she sits across the room knitting. I'm wearing a tank top, as it's another hot day in the mid-west, and he manages to hook his thumb under the shoulder strap as he's talking, blathering on and on. Mother has put her knitting down and is staring daggers in my direction. I want to tell her that I don't want this. I want to tell her that I'm tired of him – he needs to be gone from my life. He's changing me in ways she can't understand.

When he rests his head on my shoulder, still talking away, Mother has had enough. She gets up and storms over to us. I think she's going to grab him and pull him away, but instead she grabs me hard by the upper arm, her long polished nails digging into my skin, and drags me off the couch and into the kitchen.

I sputter anxiously trying to explain, to defend, to convince – but she won't hear any of it. It's not my fault Mother! It's not my fault that you choose to bring home these awful people who are starting to pay more attention to me than they are to you! I'm not interested in your men. I'm not interested in growing up too fast.

Mother won't hear any of it. Her hands are flying, hitting me about the head and face, and anywhere her blows land. In a low, gruff growl, she's calling me the most vile of names. Crying quietly, I sink down to the floor and cover my head with my hands. She's calm, her attack is methodical; she's mumbling to herself all the while. All of a sudden she stops, goes to the sink, staring out the kitchen window for a long moment. She grabs her beloved bottle and pours herself another glass. Then she walks right past me, back into the living room and fills Cleve's glass too.

Before she decides to come back, I get off the floor and run upstairs, locking myself in the bathroom. Staring at the girl in the mirror, the tear-stained, splotchy red face that I recognize less and less as time goes on, I tell her to toughen up. This is not going to change her – this is just another thing to survive – one step closer to getting out of this house and away from this town. Just hang on a little longer, I tell her. It doesn't matter what Mother does, what any of them do. You, my girl, are stronger and better than all of it. I splash cold water on my face, drying with the towel, and then I smile at my reflection in the mirror. Opening the medicine chest, I grab the scissors and crudely hack off my long blonde hair.

.VII

Mother is chasing me, down the stairs and out the front door. I run, looking back over my shoulder. She's gaining on me. It's dark and raining, and I slip in the mud. Scrambling back up to my feet, I can't see where I'm going between the rain and the tears in my eyes. I look back again - I don't see her – where is she? I reach a door and blindly open it and run inside, sitting on the ground in front of it to hold it closed. I wipe my eyes, as they adjust to the dark. Then I jump to my feet in sudden realization.

I'm in the old garage! Instantly, the stench of cigarette smoke and motor oil assaults my nose. I turn around to run out, but the door won't open – I'm locked in. I pull on it, shaking it with all my might, panic rising in my throat. Let me out, I scream. Then I hear knocking, banging – Mother is on the other side of the door, trying to get in. She wants to kill me – if she gets in here, she's going to kill me. I back away from the door, taking little steps further and further back, watching the door the rattle from the outside. It stops rattling. I stop walking, unsure what to do, where to go, now deep inside the dark garage. Then I feel it – the imperceptible sense that something is near me, right behind me...I turn around...Mother is standing behind me with a unsettling smile on her face...and beside her is a figure dressed in black, with its hand held out towards me...

I wake up bathed in sweat and panting like I had just run a marathon. Another dream, just a dream, it means nothing – it means everything. Why am I being haunted by own mind? My newly shorn hair feels foreign on my pillow, and I run my fingers through it while I wait for my heart to stop racing and try to calm down.

When Mother saw my hair the day after I had cut it, she just smirked at me. I think she was secretly happy. Now I look more like a boy, that's what she wants – she won't have to compete with a girl that looks like a boy. When Freddie saw me, he just laughed and laughed and encouraged his friends to do so too. Let them laugh... I even wear a ball cap to top off the look. I'll teach them – they'll leave me alone now...

Upsy didn't understand why I cut my hair – she always admired my long blonde locks – her mousy brown hair wouldn't grow past shoulder length. I tried to explain to her, but it seemed to upset her, so I stopped. In the long run, it doesn't change a thing about our friendship – so that's all the matters. The boys at school have stopped picking on her so much. They are leaving her alone now to make fun of my short hair. But that doesn't bother me – I ignore them or I punch them. My problems are bigger than anything that happens at school. I know I'll drop out as soon as I can.

Mrs. Delaney sees me for the first time, a few days after

my impromptu hair cut, as I walk past her place on the way home from Upsy's – she looks at me with sadness and pity. She sees the large bruise on my forehead, and thought Mother had cut my hair off in a fit of anger. She is confused for a moment when I told her, no I had cut it myself. I try to explain, but the words won't come. But then she understands, I don't have to say anymore. She clucks her tongue and brings me into her house, sits me at the kitchen table, and using her scissors, trims it up and softens the hastily cut edges, until it is at least even and looks a lot better. I hug her and thank her. She makes sure I have something warm in my stomach before I leave, looking at me sadly while I eat.

Mother married Cleve Braithwaite a month later.

<u>Years of Tragedy</u>

I

The year I turned 14 was a year of many changes, changes

I wasn't prepared for and would never recover from. I would grow up much faster than any child should; my childhood effectively ended. 14 was the year my reality shifted.

Mother had been married to Cleve for over a year now. Her last name changed for the third time by the age of 30, but I am just as glad she never bothered to change mine and Freddie's. At least we have a one constant in our lives. Like her other relationships, this one has predictably gone downhill. They argue constantly – they rarely have a nice word to say to each other. Cleve never hits her, he's not that type – he's more the smooth talker, the charmer, but when he doesn't get his way, his anger comes out in his words, saying the most vile things. Mother will fight back with words also, but she dominates him easily. She's always been prone to lashing out and violence, so she doesn't hesitate to smack him, throw something at him, or find some other way to physically hurt him. Our home is war zone, a battle ground. There is no peace here.

If I know one thing in this world, it's that I never want to have children. I understand, first hand, how children can suffer, can be neglected until they feel unwanted, and how being brow beaten and torn down every day can change a person – alter their potential until they are a mere shell of what they could have been. No one has ever taken care of me properly, shown me unconditional love, so I have never learned how to take care of someone else. I'm too busy, too consumed with taking care of myself. I have to save all my resources, all my strength for me. No one else is going to make sure I make it in this world. Yes, it may be selfish, but it's more like self preservation. It's the only thing I know – the only thing my mother ever taught me. Freddie and I have felt the sting of Mother's mistreatment since day one and it's hardened us. Maybe Freddie can turn it around and save himself. It seems like, underneath the tough exterior, he might actually be a more sensitive soul than me. When he grows up, maybe he'll be able to stop the cycle of abuse for himself. But I fear, and I feel deep in my heart, that the only legacy Mother will leave me is dysfunction – and I have no desire to bring a child into that dysfunction. If I ever do end up with such a burden, Lord help that child.

We don't have a television set, like most everyone else.

But we do have a radio, and I'm able to lose myself in the music to escape – even if just for a few moments. Music becomes a way to cope, a little reprieve from the madness around me. When I'm in the house alone, which is rare, I turn up the radio and sing at the top of my lungs. At night, I hug my little transistor radio tight next to my ear to drown out the sounds of Mother and Cleve arguing and sing along quietly. I can't sing worth a lick, but that doesn't bother me. I fall in love with lyrics and melody, but I won't ever be a singer. My dreams of California, of Hollywood, remain just as strong though. I'll get there one day, I know I will.

The arid weather and wind of late summer days whips up dust storms something fierce. Upsy and I tire of wiping the sand out of our eyes and the hair from our faces. We settle down around the kitchen table in her busy, little house and carefully thread beads onto thin strips of yarn to make friendship bracelets. With great concentration we make each other colourful treasures – mine is pink and white for her, and I add a little charm of a ballerina that I find in a box of junk that her mother lets us play with. Upsy's fervent wish is to be a ballerina. She spins and

twirls, dancing all over the house, all over the yard –
never needing music – she dances to the melodies she
creates in her head. Her Mother can't afford to pay for her
lessons, so she teaches herself and I am her audience. Her
bracelet for me is in bold strong colours - purples and
blues and reds. She says this is how she thinks of me – as
having strength and confidence. Little does she know it's
born out of necessity and the will to survive. This world is
a harsh place and I have to be strong, there's no other
choice.

I thank the universe every day for Upsy – she is, and
always has been my saving grace. Without even realizing
it, she saves me from myself, from my own self
destructive thoughts. I don't even consciously know how
much I depend on her. She listens to my thoughts and fears
without judgment. She encourages my dreams of fame
and stardom – she actually believes I can do it. If I ever
have doubts or fears on my journey to becoming a star, I'll
think of Upsy's unwavering belief in me and I'll do it for
her. She can come with me. I'll pull us out of this
poverty-stricken life and we'll never look back. I'll save
her, the same way her very presence saves me. For the

rest of my life, I will never experience a friendship as strong and as close as I have right now.

II

If the town folk have even the slightest bit of respect for us, it is certainly all lost that Autumn when Uncle Mink is arrested. It was all over the newspapers, day after day, every little detail exposed to the world. We live in a small town, and everyone knows Uncle Mink is Mother's brother. The kids tease me and Freddie at school. We are being forced to pay for someone else's sins.

A woman Uncle Mink was spending time with, the kind that you have to pay for time, went missing after last being seen with him. Police are investigating her disappearance ardently, even though she is from the fringes of society, because her father holds a well respected position as postmaster in town. Darla Watkins was born and raised in our little town, indeed she is only 4 years older than me. I knew her somewhat from school, before she dropped out three years prior, when she was not even 16. She had a seemingly normal middle class working family and normal upbringing looking in from the outside – but I know all too well the secrets that hide behind closed doors. Whatever her reasons, Darla's life veered horribly off course. She started hanging around with bad people and the soon after the rumours started flying that she was "one of those girls". I didn't know what that meant. I only knew that mother cuffed me upside the head for waving at her one day as she stood out on the street. Mother thought Darla was so beneath her, but ironically, the day we saw her in town all those years ago, the day Mother looked down her nose and clucked her tongue at Darla calling her scum, Mother was on her way to talk to Children's Services after someone once again reported our bruises.

Uncle Mink's trouble snowballed and although Darla has not yet been found, he's now also being investigated for the death of another young girl whose body was recently found in a swamp in the woods. Mother says Uncle Mink isn't even guilty, and that the police are trying to railroad him, to pin their unsolved crimes on him and make him a scapegoat. Mother says it's an election year and the Mayor and Chief of Police are just trying to bolster their reputations. She makes bold claims due to her loyalty to

Uncle Mink, the only relative she has that she gets along with. He is her source of support, both emotionally and even monetarily at times, and now that's been taken away from her and she's panicking. She is livid, but the emotions are more about worry for herself. Regardless, there is no way she can help him. He remains in jail because there is no money to bail him out.

Uncle Mink's case proceeds to trial in early winter, when Darla's body is found floating in the icy river, near the swamp where the first body was found. It is reported that there is enough evidence to charge him, although they don't comment on what evidence there is. Indeed the headlines roar soon after when Uncle Mink confesses to both crimes. Mother insists he only did so to make a deal with the Prosecution, to save himself from the death penalty. Our family is treated like pariahs, as though we too, are responsible for these girls' deaths. Mrs. Delaney and Upsy remain my support system, they don't treat me any differently, but the townspeople paint us all with the same brush. The Brewer family, always good for nothing, are now outright scorned and persecuted.

Someone is calling my name. It's faint and I can barely hear it, but when I open my bedroom window, it's louder – coming from somewhere outside. It's a familiar voice, but I can't place it. It sounds like someone needs help. I rush outside in my bare feet, the ground cold beneath them, but it hasn't snowed yet. I'm calling, "Where are you?" But no one is answering. I'm wandering around the yard, unsure of what is happening when I hear faint crying coming from behind me. I turn towards the garage; it's most certainly coming from there. The quiet sobs and calls for help continue. I don't move a muscle – I don't want to go near the garage - it's dangerous there, it's bad in there. My name is called again, louder this time, and the voice is so familiar... I inch towards the garage, looking around to make sure I'm alone. I see no one. The acrid smell of cigarette smoke and motor oil reach my nose, as I place a hand on the door and hesitate just a moment, peering into the blackness through a knothole. An eye is looking back at me and I jump back in surprise. The door swings open in front of me and the black, faceless figure that haunts my dreams stands in front of me menacingly. I'm frozen in place, my mouth wide open in shock. The figure moves aside and I see ... me.. I see me!!

I'm lying on the floor in the garage with only an old grey wool blanket covering me and I'm crying for help. The me on the ground – it's head turns and looks right at me and screams "RUN!"

The dreams are becoming more frequent, more vivid. When I wake up, usually bathed in a cold sweat, for a few moments I can't even tell if I'm awake or not. I need to find a way to stop these dreams before they drive me mad. I need to get away, I need to run, to outrun these dream...to find somewhere there's peace and where I won't be haunted any longer. I don't know it yet, but I will spend the rest of my life trying to escape the evil conjured up by my own mind.

III

As Uncle Mink's trial drags on, none of us go into town much anymore. Mother sends Cleve to do all the errands; she doesn't want to be seen. The townspeople can't possibly think any worse of her now. The whole thing is creating even more tension between herself and her husband. She's on edge and anxious all the time, even quicker to lash out at Freddie and I – to take her anxiety and anger out on us.

Freddie can't handle any of it anymore. He leaves the house one morning and he never returns, taking only his backpack. His empty room saddens me every time I walk past it. Mother rages at first, calling him names and threatening to kill him under her breath. But then a calm settles over her and it seems she's content with him being gone. One less burden, I suppose. She doesn't have a clue where her son is, but she never calls the police. After all, he just turned 18, he's an adult. Good riddance to him, she says, he better never come back if he knows what's good for him.

He won't be coming back. He never said goodbye to anyone, but he left me a note. He slipped it under my door when he slipped away in the wee hours of the morning. The note is short, but packs a punch: "Goodbye sis. I wish I could take you with me, but we will see each other again. I'm sorry I couldn't save you." Underneath is a phone number with no explanation. Maybe that's his ultimate destination, maybe it's a friend's number – whatever it is, it is my only link to him and I will keep it safe and hidden. He has hopped on a bus and is heading South. Much later, I will learn that he ended up in Tennessee, tagging along with a girlfriend who is following her dreams, determined to become a country music singer. Ultimately, she wouldn't succeed and he would go on and forge his own, surprisingly normal life. But for now, I'm jealous of his escape and I'm itching to do the same – I want to follow my own dreams, just like his girlfriend. But now is not the right time. I wouldn't speak to Freddie again for many years, but we will see each other again in the future; and this time he *will* save me. But I get ahead of myself yet again.

Eventually, Uncle Mink is convicted, sentencing happens in late Spring. He's sentenced to life in prison, a surprise to no one. Mother wails at the news, having lost her only real friend. She has no support system, she only has Cleve, and that relationship is not healthy. She tries to lean on me, but it's too late to develop a kinship with me now. She has alienated me for too long. The only thing I feel towards her is contempt. I'm not interested in being her friend.

It is early summer, where crisp mornings turn into hot afternoons. In early June, Upsy and I put our bathing suits on under our clothes and head for the river. We bring only our towels, planning to stop at Mrs. Delaney's after the first swim of the year, to warm back up and hopefully get some food. Mrs. Delaney has been feeding both of us more and more lately. Both our families are suffering pretty bad this year; there's just not enough money. Cleve and Mother fight about it constantly. She berates him for not being a good provider. He tells her to go get a job, then mocks her, saying that no one would ever hire her in this town because her brother is a murderer. The worst fights happen when they've been drinking. They seem locked together in a never ending dance of dysfunction.

The sun is high as Upsy and I make our way down to the river. We lay our towels in the grass at the water's edge and lay down, squinting up at the sun and clouds. Even though spending time with Upsy always lightens my day and brings me the only real peace and joy I experience in my life, the mood today is sombre, even quiet. The shadow that Uncle Mink's crimes have cast over my family covers me like a thick blanket. Upsy is always in tune with my feelings and she, too, is melancholy. Ever since this thing with Uncle Mink happened, it seems like she's been wanting to tell me something. Sometimes she opens her mouth to try, but promptly closes it again. I don't push her or pressure her. She's a quiet, sensitive sort, the perfect foil to my loud and brash personality, so I wait for her. She'll come around. Maybe sooner than I'm expecting.

Even though we are ready to swim, there's a bit of a nip in the air and we are waiting until the sun warms our skin enough to make the water look inviting. We alternate between talking quietly and not talking at all. We want to swim but there is something hanging in the air between us, which I'm not really aware of, that stops us from jumping into the water, giggling and laughing, and splashing each other like we normally would. I blame it on my inability to pull myself out of my sombre mood, but Upsy has other reasons.

I tell her how it's even more difficult in my house now, with Freddie gone and Uncle Mink's incarceration casting a pall over the family, over my mother especially. Upsy listens, as she always does, as I vent and even cry quietly. I tell her how hopeless I feel sometimes, how I don't know how I'm going to survive here long enough to make my escape. She remains silent, her eyes never leaving my face, as I explain how bad my dreams are becoming, how they are scaring me and I don't understand what they are trying to tell me. I wake up disoriented and scared during the night more often than not, and it's exhausting. It makes me afraid to go to sleep. I tell her about Cleve and Mother, yet another bad marriage that spills over to me, making it impossible to just live a normal life. I'm just exhausted with the constant fighting, yelling, drunkenness and abuse between them, and towards me. I really don't know how much longer I can go on but yet, something keeps me fighting to survive. For some reason, I'm a survivor, but the urge to run is becoming hard to resist. It's all so overwhelming and I just talk and talk, until I have nothing left to say. It feels good to get it out of my head, out of my heart, but I do feel bad for dumping it all on Upsy's sensitive shoulders.

Upsy looks away then, back up at the sky and takes a deep breath. She's ready to spill her own heart, but I'm not expecting what she's going say. Without looking at me even once, Upsy tells me something I never want to hear, something that hurts me deeply, something that confuses me and angers me. I'm angry at Upsy and I don't know why, because I'm actually angry for her. My emotions are colliding and I'm not handling it well at all.

Upsy tells me quietly of the day that Uncle Mink drove us to school. She was so excited getting to sit in the front of that big old convertible. It was the most exciting thing that had ever happened in her drab little life. It was something she didn't have to share with her numerous brothers and sisters, something she could treasure in her heart and tell her mother about later with a big smile on her face. That's how it was supposed to be. I didn't know any of this, as I sat in the back seat with my arms folded in huff being annoyed at having to be near Uncle Mink, I man I despised without really understanding why.

What she says next sends a resounding shock wave through my system. She tells me, almost inaudibly that while I was in the store, buying cigarettes and flipping through that magazine imagining a better future for myself, without a care in the world for those few moments....Upsy was going through the worst moments of her young life. When she finally manages to put into words what Uncle Mink had done to her in that car, in the short time it took for me to come out of the store...what he said to her, where he had put his hands, his fingers, the threats he made to her never to tell anyone, and the promises that he made that it would happen again...it was too much for her to handle. She shut right down and never spoke a word of it to anyone....until right this very minute...now that she knows he's safely in jail for a long time. Only now can she process it and share it with someone. She chooses to share it with me, but for reasons I can't comprehend, I can't empathize with her. Electric zaps race through my brain, trying to make connections that aren't quite clear, that I won't let come into focus.

I don't want to, I'm not in control of myself right now...but I actually get angry with her. How dare she put her crap on the very top of my pile of crap that is already threatening to topple over from the weight of it all. She must be lying. Why would she say such things? Trying to make me hate Uncle Mink even more than I already do...but yet...no, don't think... don't think too hard... you might not like what you find.

Before I can stop myself, I jump to my feet and yell at her. Calling her a liar, accusing her of being just another person who disparages my family. I find myself defending Uncle Mink, rattling through mother's list of defences - that he's a good man, he would never hurt anyone, he's innocent... why am I saying these things? Something else is controlling my words and actions, as my thoughts struggle to break though the chaos, take control and make everything right again. I know deep in my heart she's telling the truth, but admitting that to myself is something I'm not able to do. It's something that will break me completely. I need to protect myself at all costs, so I harden myself and rain fire down on Upsy, my best, most beloved person in the world. She's crying softly into her hands now, as I stand above her and break every single bond of friendship we've ever had. It's irreparable after what I've just done. It will never be fixed again. I'm a monster, just like my Mother.

And I storm away from her then. And by leaving her

there, I commit the single worst sin, and the biggest regret,
I will ever have in my entire life.

Upsy's body is pulled out the river later that evening, when
she fails to return home for supper.

IV

I'm inconsolable when I hear the news. Mrs. Delaney
comes to our house late that evening to speak me with me,
to tell me the story that will shatter my heart into a million
pieces. She heard Upsy's mother's cries from her front
porch, when the police came to tell her they found her
missing daughter. Mrs. Delaney ran right over, as she
knew something horrible was happening over there, but
never guessed it had anything to do with poor little Upsy.
She spent some time consoling Upsy's mother and looking
after the rest of the children until relatives arrived, then
came straight over to my house to tell me. She doesn't
understand why Upsy was swimming alone, but I can't tell
my story of shame... I can't do anything but cry. Mother
stands just outside the doorway listening. Even she sheds
a tear for Upsy and doesn't yell at me for the rest of the

day. Mrs. Delaney hugs me tight as I sob buckets of tears on her shoulder. I let her console me, as I know Mother won't.

After I left her at the river, my beloved Upsy decided to go swimming after all, without me. She was found with her foot tangled in some large rocks and logs which lay under the water on the far side of the river, towards the mouth. At least they held her in place so the current didn't sweep her downstream; she might never have been found. A small blessing, I suppose.

What must have she been thinking of me when she took that last solitary swim. She must have been confused and hurt and sad. And I did that to her. She went into the water with the weight of a million thoughts and feelings in her head, and that's what made her drown. I weighted her down as sure as if I had filled her pockets with rocks. My best friend, my only friend, my only person in this world is gone.....and it's my fault. You can only destroy that which you love.

I will carry that burden heavily within me – another

memory that I will try to outrun, another nightmare to try and get away from. I don't go to her service – I can't bring myself to see and experience the repercussions of my actions. It's my fault – and everyone will know it's my fault. They'll be able to look into my eyes and tell that I hurt Upsy so badly before she died. There is no redemption for me, I cannot be forgiven. I might as well have my own scarlet letter seared onto my chest. I hope her mother will understand why I'm not there. I'm just not capable of going through that – seeing the finality of it all. Upsy's mother sends Mrs. Delaney back over to my house to give me the pink and white friendship bracelet I had made for her. I sleep with it under my pillow, and I never mention Upsy's name out loud again. There is no one who cares as much as me anyway. But I will think of her everyday for the rest of my life.

I'm standing at the garage door again looking through the knothole. The eye from inside stares back at me and I jump back, just as I did before. The smell of cigarette smoke and motor oil fills my nose, becoming almost unbearable. The sense of deja vu is overwhelming, but there's nothing I can do that will change what is going to

happen. The garage door swings open, revealing the dark figure – this time it's grinning at me, smirking at me... this time I can see a mouth. It steps aside and I see me lying on the cold garage floor, like last time, with the grey blanket haphazardly covering me. The me on the floor looks over at me, but this time, says nothing. Something sits up on the other side of it, of me – something, someone I couldn't see until they moved. It's Upsy! Her long hair is dripping wet, water pooling around her. She's bloated and discoloured, a sickly shade of grey. She turns her head towards me, her eyes never opening, and screams,
"RUN!"

Years of Change

I

Upsy has been gone for about six months now. She is on my mind constantly, even though I don't want to think of her at all; it hurts too much. Ever since we became friends... all the days and months and years we had known each other... I thought I was the strength she needed. I believed I was the bodyguard to protect her, the assertive

one to counter her timidity, the one taking care of her....
But in her absence, I've quickly come to realize that I was
the one who needed her all along. I'm having a hard time
without her; I have no one now – no connection to anyone
or anything. I've been severed permanently, severely, and
without warning from the only person who I ever trusted,
ever confided in, ever truly felt comfortable with. I now
feel like I'm floating through life, untethered, just an
observer. And worst of all, I'm carrying the huge guilt of
my actions that day she died. The whys and what ifs
threaten to drive me insane, as my thoughts swirl around
and around; wishes, regrets and anguish entwine in a
melancholy union. And since she's been gone, my world
has changed in irreparable ways. I have become someone I
don't know. This life, this reality, has altered me,
transformed me, destroyed who I was meant to be. I'm
someone else now. I don't know this girl, and I don't like
her.

I've tried in vain several times to contact Freddie using the
phone number he left. Whenever I pass a payphone and
have a quarter, I drop it in just to try. It's become a habit
now, and as I dial, my hopes are always high. Every time it

rings and rings, never being answered, my heart is crushed. Maybe he's not settled, maybe his circumstances have changed, maybe he'll find a way to contact me. I find myself justifying, bargaining, denying – not unlike the stages of grief. But I have to keep trying, because losing my connection to Freddie would be like losing another little piece of myself, and I've already lost enough.

The relationship between Mother and I remains tense. Cleve is still paying me all sorts of unwanted attention, so I try to stay away from the house, away from him during the day. However, when he started sneaking in my room at night, I gave up. I sold my soul to the devil and float away up to the ceiling until he's gone. And that's when I stopped caring. I stop trying to save myself by dressing demurely and covering every inch of skin – because it doesn't matter what I do. I stop fretting that my hair has grown back quickly and more beautiful than ever. I start wearing what I want, rebelling and becoming someone totally different – wearing as little as I choose – tank tops, short shorts... I just don't care anymore. If that's the way Mother and Cleve see me, that's what I will be. I begin to polish my fingernails and toenails, wearing makeup and bright red lipstick. Mother wanted me to blend into the wallpaper, and I tried for the longest time, but it simply doesn't matter anymore. I deserve to stand out, to be something. So, the only thing that matters now is surviving long enough to leave them all behind, in my dust – rise above them and make a success of myself. Then they'll eat their words and what they believe about me, because I'm going to end up on top in the end – and I won't reach back down for them.

Cleve can't control me, because I could destroy him with my secret. So now he has no other choice than to watch as the boys start paying attention to me. With them, I hold the power – I control what happens to me and what doesn't. I can reject them, yell at them, punch them – everything I want to do to Cleve. And I flaunt the boys who adore me in front of mother too - I know she's jealous that she no longer garners all the male attention. I do now. It makes her feel her age, feel like a has-been. She's been used up and washed out at the young age of 34. She no longer lectures me on the evil of boys because in her eyes, in her warped view, I'm leaving her man alone.

Mother has lost all control of me, I'm just as tall as she is now. She looks at me with scorn and shame, but I glare back at her until she is the one who looks away. My anger at her oozes out of my very being, from my eyes, in my expressions, in my tone of voice – because she won't help me. She won't believe me about Cleve, she doesn't care about my nightmares, and she's affected who I am and who I could become. A wall of ice has been built between us, and it would last until both of us leave this earth.

I do have one thing in common with Mother. It is around this time, desperately seeking escape, that I begin to raid the liquor cabinet. When Mother starts to catch on, I fill the bottles with water and when she realizes that, I sneak into the store and steal my own bottles, hiding them in my room. When the store keeper almost catches me, I get the older boys to buy it for me, doing whatever I have to so that they will.... whatever they want, whatever they deem is enough to take out in trade to equal one bottle. I'm ashamed of myself, but I'm just doing what I need to get what I need to cope. I'm taking care of me the only way I know how. I don't see any other option. Besides, it feels better to be numb. I let the dependence take hold, because it is my friend now. It protects me and it never judges me, even though I judge myself. I'm able to leave behind the guilt and regret of Upsy's death and the pain of this ugly life just for a little while once I swallow enough of that poison water. Only then, can I pretend that none of it matters.

II

Cleve has done us all a favour and left Mother.

He's tired of fighting with her; he's not attracted to her anymore, and is tired of being physically abused by her in her drunken rages. He packs up his stuff, taking only his clothes and guitar, and leaves in the night.

I watch them from my bedroom window, as they fight in the yard below. She trails him to the car, yelling, screaming; then crying and pleading. She threatens, she name calls, she begs him to stay; down on her knees. For a moment, when he stops walking and turns around to face her, I'm worried that he'll change his mind and stay, but he pauses only long enough to point a finger in her face and accuse her of cheating on him and other sins. When she grabs his arm and holds him, unwilling to let him go, he yanks it away roughly and shoves her away from him. She falls backwards to the ground, her face a mess of tears and smeared makeup. Long after his car leaves in her a cloud of dust, she remains on the ground sobbing. I close the window and get into bed, falling into a sound, peaceful sleep.

With Cleve gone, a huge weight is lifted off my shoulders. I feel like I can breathe again. It is just Mother and I now. She takes his abandonment very hard. She takes to her bed, as she did when Rex died, and stays there for a few days. Then she emerges and sits on the couch, staring blindly at the tv, smoking and drinking, one cigarette, one drink, after another. When divorce papers are served to her, she retreats back to her bedroom.

I rely heavily on Mrs. Delaney during this time. I spend a lot of time with her, we do a lot of talking, as I try to work through everything in my life. I confide in her a bit, but I don't tell her the important things, the stuff that really matters...I don't tell her about what Cleve did to me and I don't tell her what I did to Upsy. I can't even make those words come out of my mouth. There's a blackness that has settled into me and I struggle to break through it just to get through every day. Instead, we talk about the good times with Upsy; we honour her with kind words and tears. She lets me cry, remaining silent while I grieve as many times as I need to.

We talk about school, and the fact that I've now dropped out. I'm 15 now, very close to 16. No one can make me go. Mother doesn't even try. Mrs. Delaney encourages me to go back, but I just don't care anymore. I have only one goal in mind and I'm just waiting for the right time...I tell Mrs. Delaney my plans to leave, go to California and become a movie star. She nods and smiles, but I can tell by her eyes that she is placating me. She doesn't think I can do it. She doesn't believe in me – but I'm not angry with her, just disappointed. I will show her too.

She comments that she noticed the change in me – the transformation from child to young woman – and she's worried that I'm becoming too much like my mother. She sees the makeup, the clothes, the boys and she can't help but express her concerns. Again, I'm not angry. I love her

for that and I assure her that I am not my mother. Things
will be better when I get away from here, from her. I'm
just biding my time. And I don't intend to have multiple
husbands and I definitely don't intend to have children. I
can't even fathom the thought. I'm far too focused on
myself. Selfishness is my defense mechanism – caring
about no one except me ensures that I will survive. If I
cared too much or allowed myself to feel all the feelings
that I keep at bay, I might as well just curl up and die. No,
I'm a fighter, so I don't have time to be responsible for
anyone except myself. That seems to ease her mind and
she's happy that I'm so self-aware, she says. Maybe there
is hope for me after all.

After our visits, I return home, lock myself in my room and
lose myself in a bottle of liquor, the same way my mother
is doing downstairs. The irony is not lost on me.

III

Walking home from Mrs. Delaney's; it's dark and damp.
The dirt road is wet, small puddles forming in the ruts and
holes. I am barefoot, walking slowly down the middle of

the road, approaching the long driveway to our house. The only light comes from the moon, and the only noise from the crickets and bullfrogs in the distance. But gradually I make out a noise behind me. A shuffling, a ruffling of sorts... I stop walking and turn around ever so slightly. My eyes take a moment to adjust to the distance, but coming into focus, there are three figures following me, catching up to me with their methodical, sluggish pace. I'm frozen in place, unable to move. The group gets closer and closer and are soon mere steps away from me - I can smell death, mixed with cigarette smoke and motor oil. One of them is Mother. Her face is blank, her eyes vacant; she shuffles along staring straight ahead, not seeing me. She is wearing a summery cotton dress and brown wedge sandals; her toenails are painted blood red. Beside mother, in the middle, is the black figure, with his unnerving smile... and this time, I can see his eyes – it's a man, his face is starting to become more detailed. He is looking at me and smirking; his eyes never leave mine, as his hand reaches out... and grabs a hold of the neck of the third figure beside him. It's Upsy. Again, looking as she must have when they dragged her body out of the river, except now the decay has taken hold, her mouth agape

and her eyes sunken and pallid. He's strangling her –
right in front of me. Still I can't move. I want to help her,
but his presence roots me to the ground and I can only
watch helplessly. Her deathly face contorts as his grip
tightens. Her hands fly up to her neck, trying to
desperately to pull his fingers off her. She chokes and
gasps for air, and as she sputters, water dribbles out of
her mouth, down her front and onto the ground, pooling at
her feet. With her last bit of air, she looks at me with
milky, lifeless eyes and yells, "RUN!" Only then can I
free myself from whatever was keeping me in place. He
drops her to the ground in heap and I start to run. I feel
like I'm weighed down, like I'm running in wet concrete... I
look over my shoulder and the man is loping after me. I
keep running with all my might... I'm running right
towards the old garage.....the garage door swings open
wide, it's beckoning me in....almost like it's calling me
home ...

I bolt upright, gasping for air, like I've just run a marathon.
I'm panting, and panicking, looking around the room with
wide eyes, sure that I'm going to see the group of three
right in front of me. I rub my eyes, shaking and crying

quietly. The dreams are getting worse, more vivid, more detailed...The hem of the summery dress, the wedge sandals and blood red toenails...why is Mother a recurring figure in this dream? And the man – who is he? What does he want? And Upsy – what is she trying to tell me? Why does she want me to run?

IV

Late Autumn is turning into early Winter. If Mother had been able to drag herself out of the deep depression that she sunk into after Cleve left, and if she had have went back to her old ways of frantically trying to find a new man to take care of her, of us....she wouldn't have lost the house.

For months, she had been avoiding the ringing phone and not opening the mail which was piling up on the kitchen counter. She was hiding her head in the sand and hoping the real world would just leave her alone...but she couldn't avoid the Sheriff who shows up at the door with the foreclosure papers. They are now pinned to our front door and we have a week to leave.

We have nowhere to go. Mother has no plans, no friends, no one to help her in a crisis. She alternates between morose moping around the house in a fog of sadness, and being in complete denial, acting like she doesn't have a care in the world. Time is counting down and I don't know what is going to become of us.

I beg Mother to let me stay with Mrs. Delaney, but Mother won't hear of it. We argue and scream back and forth long into the night. Wherever life is going to take her now, I don't want to go with her – I don't want to be dragged along on her downward spiral, on her flight to nowhere. I threaten to run away, I threaten to kill myself, I threaten to kill her ... none of it changes anything. Mother is steadfast in her plan to take me with her – and finally she knows where she's going. She has family on the East Coast – a sister in North Carolina. We are going to live with her. It's so far away from everything I know. Better the devil you know than the devil you don't, right? I can't imagine travelling with Mother only to end up in a strange place with strange people. What if her sister is just like her? What if she is worse? What if she is the nicest person, and

Mother succeeds in turning her into what she has become? I don't want to find out. We come to an impasse; Mother just shy of lashing out at me, as she raises her backhand then lowers it again. She puts her foot down, letting me know in no uncertain terms that we WILL be doing what she says. Then she goes into her room and slams the door.

I run sobbing to Mrs. Delaney's house, banging on her door, and when she opens it, I fall into her arms. She comforts me and cries with me when she finds out we are leaving. I beg her to let me stay, hide me from Mother, let me live with her. If we leave, I'll never see her again – it's too far away. She tells me that as much as she would love to have me, she cannot keep me. Mother would not allow it, would get the police involved; she would get in trouble. She explains that she's too old now - her health is declining and she'll soon be forced to leave herself and enter a nursing home. Her children are already trying to talk her into it. She won't be around for me much longer. No, she says, I'm better off to follow where this path leads me and keep surviving until I'm old enough to go off on my own. It's so close, almost within my reach. She tells me to hold on to the dream of going to Hollywood and work very hard to get there. This time she tells me I can do it, but I'm not sure if she means it, or she's just trying to give me hope. Then she leaves the room for a moment, telling me to wait right here. When she returns, she hands me a small velvet box. I open it to find a delicate gold necklace; on it, an angel with a diamond in the centre of it's halo. She says it's for me, to remember her and Upsy. I start crying all over again and hug her tight. She's been the closest thing to love that I've felt in my life, like the grandmother I never had. My heart breaks when I leave her house, knowing it will likely be one of the last times I see her. Everything is changing... it's all happening too fast.

Nearing the end of the week, Mother tells me to start packing – to take only things I need because we can only bring what we can fit in Uncle Mink's old car. He gave it to her when he realized he would never see the light of day again. We are going to be leaving most of our life behind, but at least she has finally come to the realization that she must do something, she must act. Packing only what will fit in the suitcases and bags that we own, we will be leaving this town with pretty much just the clothes on our

backs. There's nothing much I want to remember anyway.
No one will miss us.

The day before we are being evicted, Mother has one task
she wants to accomplish. She wants to go visit Uncle
Mink in prison; a two hour drive north as the crow flies.
She knows she likely won't get back this way again; it
might be the last time she ever sees him. She's mourning
the loss of his companionship, and can't seem to sever ties,
despite knowing that he is a murderer. He took the lives
of two women, yet she still feels an allegiance to him that
I don't understand. She wants me to come and visit with
her, but I refuse. She threatens, then cajoles, but I hold my
ground. I'm not going into that prison. I'm not setting eyes
on that despicable human being ever again, not after
knowing what he did to Upsy, which was the cause of our
fight on her last day of life. When Mother demands to
know why I won't visit my uncle, I blurt out exactly why,
hoping the shock of what he did to Upsy will be enough to
open her eyes. But before I can get the whole story out,
she slaps me across my face and tells me to stop lying.
She won't hear a bad word spoken about her beloved older
brother, and she refuses to believe he is anything less than

innocent of all the accusations against him. In the end, she goes alone to the prison, and I spend the day with Mrs. Delaney, trying to memorize everything about her, and soak up every ounce of the love she has for me. It will have to last a lifetime.

V

Mother doesn't vacate the house until the Sheriff shows up again at the very last minute of the very last day. She's dressed to the nines in her Sunday best, as though she's going to a cocktail party, instead of being evicted from the only home she's ever known. She holds her head high, but looks defeated nonetheless. The Sheriff escorts her out, taking her elbow and walking her towards the car, which is packed tight with our belongings. His gun is in plain view in his holster, just in case she decides to cause trouble. He knows all about the Brewer woman and her family, he has been called out to this house plenty of times for plenty of reasons, and frankly, he's happy to see us go. I follow behind, taking one last look at the house – at the garage. Maybe now that we're leaving, the old garage won't haunt my dreams anymore. Maybe the nightmares will stop all together. I never figured out the mystery, but maybe there was no mystery. If leaving the only house, the only town I've every known will make the bad dreams go away, maybe it's worth it. I hold onto that hope; it makes it a little easier to accept. Mother goes quietly, accepting her fate; she does not make a scene. The Sheriff watches us drive away, arms folded across his chest.

As we drive past Mrs. Delaney's house, she's standing in front yard, as though she's been waiting there for us. She begins to wave vigorously, trying to get our attention on our way by. I wipe a tear from my eye, as I wave back at her – a piece of my childhood, and my last connection with Upsy staying behind with her. I'm glad I'm not wearing the necklace she gave me; I've packed it in a small box in my suitcase. I wouldn't want Mother to notice it and question me, accusing me of stealing it at best...and at worst, stealing it herself to pawn it. As we leave Mrs. Delaney in the distance, I look out the passenger window, my elbow on the window frame, my chin leaning on my knuckles – I won't let Mother see me cry.

We have about a 15 hour drive to get from our Missouri town to the east coast. I've never been alone with Mother in such close proximity for such a length of time before. I've always avoided being alone with her. I developed an aversion to being near her, one that she fostered from the time that I was very small. I'm not sure how we will get along in a car for so long. We might be at each other's throats or we might ride in complete silence. For the first couple hours, Mother does stay quiet, not even turning on the radio. She broods and stares straight ahead, never taking her eyes off the road. However, once we cross over into the neighbouring state, she seems to relax a bit and her demeanour changes. Without anything else to distract her, she begins to talk.

Like we are old friends, she begins telling me about life for her when she was young. I know almost nothing about her childhood and her family. Apparently I met the aunt we are going to stay with once a long time ago, but I was too little then to remember. Her parents split up when she was young, she says. Her father taking off, never to be seen again. She found out much later that he had drank himself to death, dying of hypothermia when he passed out just outside his own front door. She and Uncle Mink remained in Missouri with their paternal grandmother, who raised her since the age of 6; the one who bequeathed her our house. Her older sister, my Aunt Magda went with her mother to the East Coast and remained there, they never once returned to visit the rest of the family. There was some sort of rift that kept them apart, Mother didn't know what. She thinks that her grandmother didn't like her mother and blamed her for her father's drinking, leaving and dying. There was bad blood amongst her family going back longer than she can remember, she sighs.

I remain quiet as she speaks, because if I say something, if I interrupt, it will alter what is happening right now. Mother will clam up and the space in the car will become silent once again and I will be left with my own thoughts; something that I find I am less and less able to cope with lately. Without noise or distraction, my thoughts swirl around in my head until the voices of worry, regret and depression begin to speak to me, yell at me, question me, degrade me – make me hate myself. My nerves and anxiety are becoming increasingly bad; medicating myself with booze is the only thing stopping it from becoming unbearable.

Mother prattles on, telling me that she hasn't seen her sister Magda for many years, since their mother died when I was little. Mother travelled with Freddie and I to North Carolina to attend the service, where she reconnected with Magda. Freddie's father had just left her, and Mother was feeling overwhelmed with two young children and no support. She stayed with Magda for quite awhile before returning to Missouri. Living with Magda wasn't easy, she confides, saying they are two very different people. Magda was quite religious and insisted that Mother attend Church with her, and that Freddie and I be baptized. Mother did what she wanted, because she wasn't ready to go home to an empty house yet. She put up with her sister's overbearing and controlling nature as long as she could. Eventually though, going back home became the lesser of two evils, and Mother left; remaining on civil terms with Magda. They had kept in touch occasionally ever since; but weren't close, in fact Mother thinks Magda is a bit of a snob, but right now she doesn't have any other options of where to go. Magda knows about Uncle Mink and what he did, and she's disgusted by it. She vowed to never speak to him again, which offends Mother greatly, but she has to put her feelings aside and try not to estrange Magda, lest she, we, be homeless. Mother says she doesn't drink, never had any children, and never married. The more I hear about Magda, the more I think maybe, just maybe, I will like her. She sounds nothing like Mother, and if there is someone who can put Mother in her place, I'd like to see it.

VI

We've been on the road for about seven hours. It is almost midnight, since Mother didn't leave until 5pm, the very last minute she was allowed to stay in the house. We are tired, getting on each other's nerves and not even half way through our journey. Mother pulls into a small motel that we come across along the highway.

I sit in the car and watch as this woman, who is dressed like she's going to high tea, walks into the dingy little motel and speaks to the unkempt, obese man at the counter, returning with a key attached to a huge orange plastic keychain.

We pull in front of our room, secluded at the rear of the motel, and bring only our necessities in with us. It is small, with barely enough room for two double beds, with an old, scuffed nightstand between them and a credenza on the opposite wall. The faded green curtains have been hanging there for a long time, with a layer of thick dust covering the top. The matching floral green bedspreads are thin and uninviting, but clean. While Mother is in the washroom freshening up, I look out the open door into the night and seriously consider running away, just running off into the night. I almost do it. I stand up and walk over, standing in the door frame and look back over my shoulder at the closed bathroom door. How easy it would be just walk out, disappear...but the only thing that stops me is that I have nowhere to go and no way to get there. It's too cold to walk or hitchhike. I'm not an adult yet, so if I'm caught, I'll just be brought right back to Mother. I need to keep biding my time until I can make my move. I'm itching to run – why else does Upsy keep urging me to run in my dreams? It takes every ounce of strength I have not to leave that motel and vanish into the dark. In the end, I close the door and continue to wait.

Mother is still in the washroom, she has the shower running, but it doesn't cover up the sound of her tears. I turn to my small bag of clothes and toiletries and unzip the top. Hidden at the bottom is a bottle of rum that Charlie Kaner bought for me, after a quick encounter in a dim alleyway, or was it behind his house? I don't even remember. I'm just glad to have it here to bring me comfort. I open the cap and take a swig. It doesn't matter that there's no ice or mix - straight is fine, the more it burns, the better. It takes away the voices in my head for a few moments. I hear Mother finishing up and opening the door, so I quickly stuff the bottle back in my bag and lay down on the bed closest to the door, crossing my ankles, fingers locked behind my head, and stare at the gypsum board ceiling. She says nothing when she comes out, so I go into the washroom, and when I come out, she's standing facing me, holding the bottle from my bag – she had seen the top of it peeking out where I'd hurriedly pushed it back in.

I stop dead in my tracks and we lock eyes. I don't know

what is going to happen now. I expect her to start yelling and lash out, maybe pummelling me into a corner at the same time. What I don't expect is for her to sigh heavily, then go retrieve two plastic cups from the bathroom and sit down on the opposite bed and pour us both a drink. I take my cup warily, still thinking this is some kind of trick, expecting the worst. She raises her cup in a toast and drinks down the shot she's poured. After more hesitation, I do the same. We finish that bottle together that night – it has been the only thing we've ever had in common; an uneasy and unhealthy alliance forms.

After a fitful, but dreamless sleep, we are up and on the road again. It is still strained between us, but an understanding seems to have developed. An awkward bond of mother and daughter, both tossed into the same storm, trying to make their way. Mother is less volatile, but still quite moody. She drives in silence, as the car struggles to warm us up in the chill of the morning.

We don't have a lot of money, so Mother buys us some sodas and a bag of chips to share at the nearest gas station, and that will be our breakfast. She is hoping to arrive at

Aunt Magda's in time for a nice, hot supper. We are only on the road a couple more hours when the car starts to sputter and breaks down. Cursing, she lets it glide onto the side of the road and puts her head down on the steering wheel. Her coping skills are not good, she's used to being taken care of, of never having to be responsible for herself; she has no idea what to do.

We are in the middle of nowhere, on a long, straight lonely road, still hours from our destination. The last sign we passed just minutes ago, said that the next town is still miles away. The car starts to get chilly within seconds. Mother turns the key trying to start it repeatedly, but it chugs and dies every time. She's angry and frustrated. Getting out of the car, she puts the hood up and looks in, as though she knows what she's looking at. Then she gets back in the car, the open hood blocking our view of the road in front of us.

We sit, waiting...waiting for what? Mother mutters under breath that this is what happens without a man in your life to take care of you. She turns to me and tells me to let this be a lesson – having a man around is more important than whether you actually love him or not. She says don't hang your hat on love, don't bother chasing it...it doesn't exist. I nod, not even realizing the influence those words are going to have on the rest of my life. It seems learned helplessness is destined to be inherited by the women in my family.

Almost as if proving her point, a truck pulls up behind us. A tall, thin older man walks up to the driver's side window, looks in at us for a moment, then walks around the front of the car to look under the hood. Mother quickly jumps out and goes over to talk to him. He looks like a kindly grandfather, white hair thinning on the top, dressed sharply in a button down shirt and blazer. I sit inside and watch, as they close the hood and stand in front of the car talking, mother gesturing animatedly with her hands all the while. She's prone to histrionics and I can tell she's on the verge of tears. The man nods his head and puts a reassuring hand on her shoulder, then returns to his vehicle and drives away. I look at her questioningly when she gets back in the car, but say nothing.

With a small, satisfied smile on her face, she tells me that

William, his name is William, is going to go up ahead and find a tow truck for us. Now that a man is in control, Mother is much calmer. He had looked trustworthy enough, but looks can be deceiving. Mother has no radar for trouble, she trusts men easily, often to her detriment. I doubted that we would ever see him again. I'm more cynical than she is, sometimes she lives in a dream world, where all men are Prince Charming and all women are princesses needing to be saved. He proves me wrong though, when he returns a short time later, followed by a tow truck from the town ahead. Mother claps her hands together and smiles, grabbing her purse and hopping out of the car.

The early winter air is crisp and cool; as the tow truck driver is hooking the car up to bring it to the garage, we sit in William's car to stay warm. Mother introduces me and he tips his hat, nodding towards me. I sit in the back and quietly watch the interaction between them. Mother is charming and friendly, gushing over him and his willingness to help us. She thanks him again and again, but then quietly admits that she has no money to pay for any of this. She turns on the tears, she knows what she's doing. She's done this before.

He's a good man, he tells her she reminds him of his daughter, and I, his granddaughter. He wouldn't leave us stranded on the side of the road, and he won't leave us without a way to get to where we're going. I've never experienced a man that is selfless and caring, so I can't help but be suspicious. Surely he'll expect something in return; nobody does something for nothing.

But as he drives us to the garage, following behind the tow truck, he begins to speak and my misgivings turn into admiration. He talks of being in the war, how he had just met his wife and had to leave her behind to go overseas. They kept in touch with spotty letters, and she waited for him. They lost contact for awhile, and she feared he had died, when he ended up in a makeshift hospital after taking shrapnel to his shoulder. His war wounds cause him chronic pain, but he says he still finds something to smile about every day. Except the day his wife died, just a few months ago. That was a dark time, he admits. He says he will mourn her every day of his life, but she lives on in their daughter, their only child. He has always taught his

daughter to do unto others, just like the Bible says. So
that's why he's helping us. It warms my heart to hear his
stories, and I wish he was my grandfather. What a different
life I might have led with someone like this in my world.
The anger that I feel about the way I was raised and the
people who surrounded me bubbles to the surface, but I
push it back down. Now is not the time. I will need all
that anger when I can harness it and use it to help me break
free.

When we get to the garage, he waits with us while the
mechanic looks at the car. It turns out to be an easy fix,
although we will have to wait awhile, because the little
place is quite busy. Mother thanks him again and gives
him a big hug, which he returns with a smile on his face.
He is pleased; he has done something good – his wife
would be proud.

After he leaves us there, continuing on his way, Mother
brings us across the street to a little diner to eat and wait. I
thought she had no money. I was told we wouldn't be
eating again until we got to Aunt Magda's. When I
question her, I'm terribly sad when Mother reaches into her

pocket and proudly shows me that she has stolen William's wallet.

VII

By the time we get back on the road, it's late afternoon. We still have 5 hours left to drive before we get to Aunt Magda's. We don't talk, but at least now she turned on the radio. She doesn't like the popular music, so she keeps it low, but at least it's a distraction. I fall asleep, lulled by the movement of the car and the sound of the tires, and it's dark when I open my eyes again. A large moon shines down, making eerie shadows on the ground.

We are pulling into a driveway; Mother says we're here. The neighbourhood is quiet; there are only a few houses scattered yards away from each other on the road; very private and unassuming. I look up at the house, which is surrounded by tall, thick hedges. The ornate outside lights at the front illuminate the front yard. Magda lives in a Queen Anne Victorian home, with three floors and large white pillars on the front porch. Many windows stare back at me like eyes, including a small, ominous attic window at the very top, all surrounded by white scalloped wooden designs. It's obviously old and could use some restoring, maybe a new roof, as shingles flap in the breeze; bricks are crumbling around the edges. It looks like a haunted house, and I shudder involuntarily.

Mother tells me to grab whatever I can carry and get moving, we'll get the rest tomorrow. I can't believe Aunt Magda lives here all alone, wondering if she's lonely, as I follow Mother to the front door. When we get there, she doesn't know whether to ring the bell or use the door knocker, so she does both. After a moment, the large wooden door opens and we are ushered into a large foyer. Aunt Magda greets mother with a brief hug, a stiff look on her face. Mother introduces me and Magda nods. As they talk, I take in not only the house, but her as well. Aunt Magda is a very thin woman, slightly older and taller than Mother, but looking every ounce the epitome of a spinster. She is wearing a plain black dress, almost ankle length, with some decorative white lace at the neck. Laying on her chest is a small cross on a long gold chain. Her blonde-turning white hair is pulled back severely in a bun; black horn-rimmed glasses perch on her nose. While talking to

Mother, Magda is looking at me, judging me, I feel. She is wondering what kind of trouble this teenager is going to be. What has she done allowing both of us in her home, her sanctuary from the outside world? She's doubting her decision, I can see it in her eyes.

Years of Revelation

I

Magda sets out the rules right away, before we are even able to go to bed the first night. In no uncertain terms, she tells us there will be no alcohol, drugs or cigarettes in this house; there is a curfew of nine o'clock on week nights and ten o'clock on weekends; there will be no cursing or fighting; suppers are promptly at 6pm and there will be nothing until the next morning if missed. And most important, if we are to be welcomed here, then I am to attend school regularly, and that is not up for debate. Mother sits beside me at the large wooden kitchen table, with her head down, as if we are both children being chastised. Magda concludes her litany of rules with saying that she attends church twice a week. We are welcome to come with her, but she won't make that mandatory, not right away anyway. She hopes, and indeed expects, that eventually we will join her.

She shows us to our rooms, up the long wooden staircase, carpeted in red and gold; the carpet is practically threadbare. I hold onto the huge wooden banister as we ascend further and further into the house. Mother and I will have rooms across the hall from one another, to the right of the staircase. Magda's room is to the left. She says her door is always closed, and we are to knock if we ever need her. She points to the washroom at the end of the corridor, says goodnight and leaves us standing in the middle of the hall.

Mother and I look at each other wordlessly; I don't think this is the welcome she was expecting from her sister. She goes into her room and quietly closes the door, looking defeated. I stand in the hallway holding my bag, just taking in the huge house for a moment. At first glance, it looks rich and opulent, but when I look closer, even in the dim lighting coming from the wall sconces, I can tell the house is in ill repair. It is hardly as grand and luxurious as it first appears. There is wallpaper peeling, wainscotting pulling off the walls, and paint flaking. Once more, I am reminded that even though things may look flawless on the surface, if you look below, you often find things are not as they appear. Magda lives in this house alone, and it is starting to fall apart around her.

Sighing, I too go into my room and close the door. Turning on the light, I am disappointed in what I see. The room is smaller than it should be for a house this size. A single bed with a wrought iron frame and headboard sits on the opposite wall beside a sizable old window; a tear in the screen flapping in the breeze. It is open a crack at the bottom, no doubt trying to air out the stuffiness; the room has obviously been closed up and unused for quite awhile. A weathered, scuffed up desk sits on the other side of the window and tall dresser stands beside the door. Besides the pale yellow curtains with a rip down the centre of one panel and a clock on the wall, there is nothing else in the room. I set my bags down and pull the window down closed, turning the rusty lock in the middle. Looking out, I can tell I'm at the back of the house; Mother must be at the

front. The clock is showing almost midnight; it's been a
long day. I lay on top of the bed, fully clothed, and fall
into a deep, exhausted sleep.

*There's a scratching noise coming from the closet. It
wakes me up; I'm disoriented, and it takes me a moment to
figure out where it's coming from. It must be mice, or
maybe a squirrel in the wall. I try to settle back down and
go to sleep, but the scratching is persistent; it has changed
from quick scratches, to long, slow scraping sounds. I get
out of bed and tip toe over the cold wood floor, pressing
my ear to the closet door. The noise continues, rhythmical
and methodical. I reach out and grab the cold brass knob,
hesitating just a moment, and slowly open the door. It
creaks, as it moves inch by inch. It's so dark, I can barely
see anything. Looking up, I spot a cord hanging low,
leading to a light bulb on the ceiling. I grab it and pull,
and the large closet lights up. Blinking, it takes me only a
moment before my eyes adjust – then I scream.... Upsy is
sitting at the back of the closet, against the wall. Long
gouges, her fingernail marks, trail down the back of the
door. She looks up at me; her eyes are opaque and her
skin, a mottled grey. Her mouth opens, she's trying to*

speak, it's garbled, "Don't you know?" I shake my head and back away. She stands up in the closet, illuminated eerily by the light above her.... and she takes a shuffling step towards me. Her mouth opens wide and she yells, "RUN!"

II

Someone is screaming. It's loud, it's hurting my ears. My eyes bolt open. It's me! I'm screaming! And I can't stop! Mother sits on the bed, shaking me by the shoulders; when I don't stop screaming, she slaps me across the face. Aunt Magda is standing behind her near the door, her hand in a fist, pressed to her mouth. My cheek is stinging, I'm awake now. I stop screaming abruptly, embarrassed but trembling from the nightmare.

"What on earth....," Aunt Magda peers at me.

Mother knows what is happening. She hasn't had to witness one of my nightmares in a long time, but she knows.

"Must just be the stress of the move Magda. Go back to bed, I'll handle this." She looks over her shoulder at her older sister.

"Oh my...," Magda is rattled, but she backs out of the room, fanning herself with a hanky and closes the door.

Mother turns back to me with fire in her eyes, "You must never do that here again! Do you understand?" She growls.

I try to tell her I can't control it, that I don't want it. I try to tell her that I'm terrified. That Upsy followed me here. Leaving home did not stop the night terrors like I was so desperately hoping it would. I don't know how much longer I can stand the dreams. I don't know what it all means. I need help. I'm rambling, words tumbling out of me fast and jumbled. But Mother doesn't want to hear it. She growls in a harsh whisper, saying that if Magda throws us out because of my behaviour, we will be on the streets, don't I understand that? What she doesn't understand, is that I didn't ask for any of this. I didn't ask to move from one godforsaken place to another, I didn't ask for Upsy to come visit me in my sleep, and most of all, I didn't ask to be born...

Mother goes back to her room as the sun is just starting to rise. The room brightens, taking away the last vestiges of panic and fright. I lay awake, unable to get back to sleep, wondering...why did Upsy follow me here...what is she trying to tell me...when will it stop?

Later, I'm dressed and heading downstairs. I'm still tired from the events of the night, from the long trip, from fear of the unknown. In the light of day, the house appears more garish than regal. The fancy looking furniture is worn and tacky, golds and burgundy, mixes of patterns and shades...oversized, heavy curtains adorn every window keeping out most of the sunlight. There are religious pictures hanging on the walls and religious icons sitting on the shelves. A big cross hangs on the wall in the sitting room. After their mother died, Magda holed herself up in this house, sequestering herself from the outside world, except for her weekly trips to church. The house is neat and tidy enough, but it's dying from the inside out. It needs some care and restoration to return it to it's previous luxury. I take it all in, as I follow the voices leading me to find Mother and Magda in the kitchen. They turn and look at me as I walk in.

Mother glares at me until I feel the need to apologize for the commotion the night before, but that's all I say. I can't promise it won't happen again. Now that Upsy is here, I'm sure it's just a matter of time before the rest of the bad dreams and the dark figure returns as well.

Magda nods and clears her throat, straightening her back tall in her chair. The first thing she says is that I am expected to dress respectably in this house. I look down at my t-shirt and jeans and look back at her, confused. Too tight, she says, too low cut. And the makeup has to go. No one will look like a harlot here. I look at Mother, who looks down at her plate. I think both of us are going to have trouble adjusting to this move. I'm angry, but I say nothing, since Mother's patience is already tested from the night before. I eat breakfast quietly and plot my escape.

III

Right away, I'm enrolled in school, per Magda's insistence. Mother is determined to adhere to Magda's every stipulation. She's terrified of being kicked out of Magda's house and being responsible for herself. I guess I can't blame her. She doesn't have any skills, she'd never get a job even if she wanted one. She is completely dependent on others. Out of her own environment, she's no longer the angry, volatile mother I'm used to. She is disoriented, uncomfortable and uncertain. But she does break one of her sister's rules – she's still drinking. She hides her bottle in her room, but not from me. She knows I won't tell on her, because I rely on it too. So the two of us cover for each other, bonding over our addiction, drinking in secrecy, usually at night after Magda has gone to bed.

I stand in front of the school on my first day, observing everything and everyone around me. Students and teachers alike have taken a moment or two to stare at the new girl. It's a small town and a small school, maybe a couple hundred students. Not too many new people come around, so I'm a novelty; people are nosy. Entering the building, the first place I head is to the washroom. I learned very quickly that the way I will cope in my new environment is to be sneaky. What Magda doesn't know, can't hurt her. I change from my conservative clothes into what I'm used of wearing and put on the makeup I'm no longer allowed to wear at home. I will exist here on my own terms or I won't exist at all.

Looking at my schedule, I find my first class and walk in late. Everyone turns around to look at me, the boys take notice. The tall, skinny teacher with a long, ski slope nose and a tan corduroy blazer stops talking and looks over the top of his glasses at me, but says nothing. I take a seat in the back row. I'm not interested in anything that's happening, I'm just here killing time. This change in my life is not ideal and I need to leave soon. I just need an opportunity.

The teacher is called out of the classroom, and the class erupts in chatter. Most talk amongst themselves, girls forming their usual cliques. Boys throw things at each other and keep taking sly glances at me. I'm about to get up and walk out, give up on the whole thing and see how long it takes to face Magda's wrath when she realizes I haven't been going to school, when the girl beside me starts talking to me. I look at her – she has flaming red hair, tied back with colourful bandana headband. She's wearing bell bottom jeans and a bohemian shirt, and tells me her name is Marva.

If it wasn't for Marva, I never would have went back to that school. Marva is the closest I've felt to friendship since I lost Upsy all those years ago. I have gone without any connection to another human being for so long that I almost weep with relief that I've found another friend. Marva is sassy and a smart aleck; she curses like a sailor. Her big mouth and sarcasm get her in trouble frequently at school. She's into music and fashion, always dressed stylish with lots of makeup and long fake nails polished in bright red. She really wants to be a hair stylist; maybe a make up artist, so I let her practice on me. She always has a boyfriend, usually a new one every other week. The boys love her, the teachers don't. She is me. She is my twin. For all that she is, she'll never be Upsy. Poor Upsy who never got to grow up, who died in fog of sadness after I hurt her more than her secret did; after I rejected her for her truth. She haunts me now, but I deserve it.

Marva comes from a fractured family too. Her mother died when she was little; she has run wild ever since. She lives with her father, who has no control over her at all. She tells me she never got along with him, and had lost all respect for him last year. When I ask why, she gets quiet and tells me that she had fallen in love with a young man named Luther, and her father had run him off for the sole reason that he was black. She loved Luther more than anything – she would have married him. But her father did not approve of race mixing, and that's when she discovered he was a racist. She says she will never forgive him. She throws parties when her father is working nights at the quarry. When he's home, she sneaks out to parties after he's asleep. And I follow her. I've discovered that, since my room is at the back of the house, I can sneak in and out easily through that old window that opens wide and doesn't quite close right. I just lock my door, then climb out the window, close it lightly and climb down the tv antenna that is off to side. It was hard to find my footing at first – I almost fell once, but now I do it easily. I come and go as I please. Neither Mother nor Magda has ever come to check on me. As long as I'm back before daybreak, I can have a life of my own.

Lately it's been more and more difficult to tolerate Magda. Her piousness grows every day; she's always trying to force her religion down our throats. She walks around carrying a Bible and never misses an opportunity to spout out Bible verses to Mother or I whenever she feels the situation calls for it. I have come to realize pretty quickly, however, that Magda is all bark and very little bite. She sets down rules, but doesn't have much follow through when they are broken, so I'm starting to bend those rules a bit. Magda will walk around in a huff mumbling to herself and praying in her room, but she doesn't kick us out. She said once that she was afraid to die alone in this house; it is her greatest fear. With us here, her anxiety is diminished.

Mother tries her best to follow the rules. At first, drinking privately in her room at night is enough, but slowly and surely, bits and pieces of the old Mother, the real Mother are coming out. A few months into our stay Mother starts going out to the local bars, coming home reeking of alcohol and men's cologne. She's lonely and she's always been a social creature; she's not happy with this cloistered lifestyle. She obeys the curfew at first, however, one night she comes in late and Magda is incensed, waiting for her at the door. I watch her from upstairs, pacing and muttering, clutching that Bible so tight her knuckles are white.

"1 Corinthians 6:10 – 'Nor thieves, nor the greedy, nor drunkards, nor revellers, nor swindlers will inherit the kingdom of God', Louise!" She bellows as soon as Mother walks through the door.

Mother is startled and caught off guard. She apologizes profusely, scared of her sister's vehemence. Magda puts the fear of God into her that night, following her up the stairs to her room, yelling that she was going to go to Hell and will burn for all eternity. Magda continues to holler and threaten, then begging and pleading for Mother to save herself, trying to convince her that she needs to repent and pay for her sins. I go to bed, listening to the lecture go on and on long into the night.

That event marks a turning point; things are different after that night. It's starts slowly, with Mother listening attentively, like an apt pupil, while Magda talks in sermons, preaching about Heaven and Hell and salvation. She follows her older sister around obediently, hanging on her every word. It is inevitable, it's the next step...she easily gets drawn back into the Church. She starts going to help Magda volunteer, meeting all the other parishioners. She attends prayer meetings and Bible studies. Soon after, Mother too, begins carrying a Bible around. Magda has succeeded in converting her, using Mother's fears of her own past behaviours to frighten her into compliance. It wasn't a difficult conversion, since Mother also went through a period of being very religious when I was little, punitively so. I'm afraid of where this is going. Mother always takes everything to the extreme, and this will be no different.

However, for all her attempts at being Godly, in the end, Mother remains nothing more than a hypocrite – she still drinks in her room, still hiding her bottle on top of the wardrobe. She also continues to sneak out of the house at night, except now she is more stealthy; waiting until Magda is sleeping, making sure to return before she's awake. During the day, she is a demure, obedient sister;

but at night, she's the Mother I know. The dichotomy between the two confuses me, I never know how to take her. Deep down, I'm sure it's all an act. She's ingratiating herself with Magda, ensuring her security, hiding her true self, so her sister won't know the person that she really is.

IV

As my world at home continues down a path of righteousness, my outside world is at least more interesting. Marva and I continue to spend a lot of time together, and get into a lot of trouble together. In school, we are known as troublemakers, even bullies. In Marva, I've found a kindred spirit – someone who is also struggling to make her way in this world, and we do whatever we can to cope. We have nothing in common with the kids from nuclear families, with mothers and fathers to love them, taking care of their every need, buying them whatever they want. The majority have no idea what it's like to live as we live, and we are unrepentant in how we choose to survive.

Marva is the only person who knows my secret about

Cleve. I told her one night, after we had been drinking too much. It poured out of me like a confession. Tears ran down my face without me even realizing it, as I bared my soul. Marva cried with me, and when we were sober, we never spoke of it again.

For the most part, I've been able to keep my home life and outside life completely separate. I've become an expert at sneaking out of the house, at hiding my makeup and clothes until I get to school so I can change in the school washroom - then taking it all off and changing back into my more appropriate clothing before I go back home. I have Magda's schedule down pat, she never strays from her wake/sleep cycle and her morning routine. As long as I'm back in the house before dawn, I can do as I please. Mother is having her own struggles, so she is paying no attention to mine. Not being under anyone's thumb is a freedom I've never known before.

However, my two worlds collide on a weekend afternoon in late Spring when Marva and I get caught for shoplifting at one of the local stores. We raised the ire of an attentive cashier who followed us around and saw Marva put a pair of hoop earrings in her pocket, She stopped us at the door and called for Security who searched us and our bags, finding other unpaid for items, including more jewellery, a pack of gum, lipstick...nothing important, but stolen nonetheless.

We are taken to the police station, being in a police car, in our minds, is pretty exciting. When our parents are called, we sit in a long row of chairs, waiting. I don't know what Mother is going to do. I'm nervous, but at the same time I don't care. It's only a matter of time now before I can get away from her for good. I'm just waiting for an opportunity to present itself. Let her do her worst; nothing she does matters.

To my dismay, she shows up with Magda in tow, holding her Bible. She speaks quietly with the policeman who then releases me to her, just as Marva's father is arriving. We wave to each other, smiling slyly. We know whatever happens, we will carry on as usual, this friendship will not change. If anything, it has been strengthened, as we have bonded over this teenage rite of passage.

They are both quiet as mice, until we reach the car. Mother, with her hand on the door handle, throws her head back and talks to the sky, "Oh Lord, let me not be put to shame, for I call upon You; let the wicked be put to shame." She wails dramatically.

"Psalms 31:17," Magda nods, looking at me.

And I hate that Magda has turned Mother into this, a religious zealot, like herself. I haven't figured out if it's all an act for Magda's sake, or if she really believes what she is spouting, but regardless, it makes her more incorrigible than ever.

All the way home, I am threatened with brimstone and fire. Magda continues to quote the scriptures, while Mother yells angrily about bringing shame upon her and disrespecting Magda's hospitality. When we get back to the house, she demands that I kneel in front of the makeshift shrine that sits in the corner of Magda's living room and pray for forgiveness. I scoff at her, at which point she yells at me, "The eye that scorns to obey a mother will be picked out by the ravens and eaten by vultures!" Another verse from her Bible.

I can't control myself, I'm so angry. She's trying to intimidate me, and I won't let her. Her eyes blaze fury, but she no longer strikes out at me. I am taller and bigger than her now, so she knows she can no longer control me physically. We are in a war of words now. She tells me that I am never to see Marva again, and I snort derisively, warning her that she better stop, or she might not like the secrets of hers I can reveal; things she might not want her sister to know. This makes her take a step back and close her mouth. That's when Magda hops into the fray, threatening to kick me out on the streets. Her voice rising thunderously, shaking her fist to the ceiling, as she calls me a sinner, a evildoer, a criminal...

They are both surprised when I spew their own rhetoric back at them, "For all have sinned and fall short of the glory of God! Romans 3:23!" They are not the only ones who have studied the Bible. After listening to her go on and on every day, constantly preaching, I finally picked up the Book myself – know your enemy they say – and it paid off in spades at this very moment because the argument instantly ceases – they are both speechless. Magda sniffs and leaves the room, nose in the air. Mother follows, but not before snarling at me that I'm walking on thin ice, and one more infraction and she will let Magda throw me out of the house, and then I'll be forced to fend for myself. She has no idea that I plan to do just that as soon as I can.

The atmosphere in the house remains tense. I still haven't figured out how to get myself to California yet, and I need more time. I can't risk getting kicked out right now; the timing is not right. I try to fly under the radar, but Mother continues her overt disregard for all that she preaches. The blatant risks that she is taking by sneaking in and out, dressed up like a harlot lead me to wonder if she has met someone after her many forays to the bars and nightclubs. I could threaten to tell Magda her transgressions, but I don't. I just wait and watch; I have patience. Mother will be her own undoing. Something is going to happen, it's just a matter of time.

Marva and I have been skipping school, spending our days hanging out around town, smoking and drinking in the alleys. We meet a couple of older guys who introduce us to pot and hash; we experiment a bit. It makes us feel grown up and untouchable, brave and carefree. Although it would be so easy to lose myself in that world, drugs are not really my thing. I need to maintain some semblance of control over myself and my actions if I'm going to get where I'm going. Besides, my vice will always be alcohol. However, it does present Marva and I with a money making opportunity which I jump at. We begin selling, becoming mules for our new "friends", and we start to make some real cash. I know we are taking a huge risk, and getting caught could derail everything I'm working towards, but the lure of easy money is just impossible to give up. We certainly aren't making anything more than pocket change at this point, but it's all adding up, every dollar counts, every deal counts. While Marva spends her money on make up and hair dye, I am squirrelling it away in a small box hidden deep under my bed, saving it to fund my escape. It's getting closer – I can almost taste it.

Once in a while, the two of us hop on a bus to the city, which is less than an hour away. We spend a few hours there, hanging out after selling to the city customers. Then we hop back on the bus in time to arrive back in town by the time school is out.

It is in the city that I discover the way I will get away from Mother and this life – the stepping stone to my escape. We come across a billboard ad looking for models. It doesn't contain a lot of information, just a picture of a beautiful girl, a phone number and address, divided into separate tabs along the bottom of the page. I take a number and stuff it into the pocket of my jeans for later. Do I dare? Can this be the sign I've been waiting for? Has my way out of here has finally appeared? If I take this chance, I could soon be looking at North Carolina in the rear view mirror and creating my own life.

V

There's a sharp knock at my bedroom door. It's the middle of the night, and I'm roused out of a deep sleep. I get out of bed and open the door. Upsy is standing there, her head tilted to one side, looking at me with those dead, questioning eyes. She reaches out her hand and wants me to follow her. I take her hand in mine, feeling the decaying skin sloughing off, but I smile because it reminds of the old days when we would hold hands skipping down the road or dancing in circles in the fields until we fell down with laughter. She seems to sense the memory, and tilts her head to the other side, smiling slightly. But her smile quickly fades, as her attention is drawn to something behind her, something I cannot see or hear. She pulls me forward and out the door. We step out into the yard, and when I look behind me, I see that we just walked out of my old childhood house. I'm back in Missouri; Upsy has brought me home. She's pulling me across the yard and towards the old garage. No, no, no... I beg her. I try to pull away, but her strength is unexpected. I can't get out of her grasp. Her grip tightens, and I am powerless to stop her. When we get to the garage, she pulls the door open and pushes me inside. I fall to my knees on the hard, cold cement floor. Instantly, the smell of motor oil and cigarettes fills in the room. She stands beside me and points forward. I see the dark figure, the man, standing in the middle of the garage. A car, with the convertible top open, is jacked up, off to the side. His eyes bore a hole through my soul, and I feel a pain I've never felt before deep in my heart, deep in my body...his lips are sneering, the face is starting to become clear, to come into focus... I slam my eyes shut. I don't want to see! Make it go away, I yell at Upsy. I turn and look at her, begging her silently to make it all stop. She kneels down in front of me, her face close to mine, and puts her hands on either side of my head. Through the scent of death, I can sense her sadness... and also... her fear? She twists my head until I'm facing the figure again, forcing me to look forward, forcing my eyes to stay open.   There are voices, laughter...a loud crash. I jump up, out of Upsy's grasp, push to the garage door open and take off into the night. Behind me I hear Upsy yelling, "RUN!"

I jerk awake with a guttural grunt. Bolting upright and breathing heavily, I look around the room. My eyes dart all over, making sure Upsy is not standing in any of the darkened corners; making sure there are no dark figures beside me or above me. Calming down, I realize that I'm in my bed in Magda's house. The clock says three a.m. Everything is back to normal. I flop back onto the pillow, trying to settle my pounding heart. Upsy, why are you here? Why are you tormenting me? I'm sorry, I'm so sorry... If I could take back every cruel word I said that day, every word that broke your heart, I would. If I could trade places with you, I would do so in a heartbeat. I would walk down to the river right now, and walk into that water over my head and take a deep breath if it would bring you back. I never wanted you to die. I mourn you every day, but you're scaring me. What can I do to make you leave me alone, to help you rest in peace? Mulling over these questions as I fall back asleep, a little voice in the back of my head knows she is trying to tell me something.

VI

Spring turns into summer. I haven't made it back to the city yet to follow up on the modelling ad, but I plan to, I just haven't had a chance. Mother's descent into madness comes to an abrupt halt when she admits to me that she has met someone. Months of sneaking out at night has led her to a way out of Magda's clutches. She no longer has to follow the rules of her overbearing sister. She's ready to move out and live with her new boyfriend; they have been talking about marriage. She's like a schoolgirl, as she's telling me, giggling and blushing, proud of herself. For a moment, I'm afraid that she's going to leave me behind;

that's she's going to sneak off in the night and abandoned me at Magda's. But she surprises me, saying that Jim knows that she has a child and he's fine with that. We are moving out, and although I'm nervous about possibly jumping out of the frying pan and into a fire, there is no other choice but to follow her.

Magda does not take the news well. She follows Mother around her room as she is packing, berating Mother for her duplicity and for taking advantage of her. She says she did not have to be kind and accept us into her home, and this is how we repay her. She was trying to save our souls, she says, if we leave this house we are doomed to burn in Hell. My bags are packed and I stand in the doorway, quietly watching the scene unfold. Magda stops ranting and turns on me. There is no need for pretenses anymore, I'm dressed the same as when I first entered her home. The tight clothes, the makeup, I can just be me again, and Magda has no recourse.

She smirks and calls out, "Leviticus 19:29, do not profane your daughter by making her a harlot," She turns back to Mother, "The apple does not fall far from tree Annie!" She continues on, blaming Mother for how I've turned out, for my own misdeeds and sins... the thing is, she's not wrong.

In end, Magda watches us leave, her relationship with her sister is severed, unsalvageable. She is truly alone now, in a prison of her own making. I won't miss her.

Mother has moved us in with Jim. He's older than her by several years, how many, I couldn't guess. He's a retired electrician, having owned his own small business – just himself and two other employees, but it was enough to ensure his financial stability. No wonder Mother is proud of herself, if she can make this relationship last, she will have secured her future and will no longer have to worry about the poverty that plagued her all our lives. Jim is imposing and authoritative, a tall, big man with deeply etched lines on his face. His heavy eyebrows, unnaturally dark compared to his thinning grey hair, shadow hard, stern eyes. It's clear from the beginning that he is used to being in charge; he is dominant and domineering. Mother is used to being the one in control, but she is going to need to take a backseat to this man. He lets us know, in no uncertain terms, that this is his house and he rules the roost; he makes all the decisions. His opinion is the only one that counts. It is strange to see Mother displaced from her role, but oddly satisfying.

However, his pomposity quickly becomes hard to bear. He has an opinion about everything, is always right about everything; he expects to be served, obeyed. His overbearing personality becomes too much for me. We begin to butt heads, arguments quickly become yelling matches. Mother sits quietly on the sidelines, never getting involved. She will not risk her place in this relationship, so I'm on my own to fight my own battles. Jim mocks, taunts, and lashes out with an occasional backhand or slap across the face. Through it all, Mother remains silent.

I come home one afternoon to find that Mother and Jim have been married by the Justice of the Peace.

Husband number four.

VII

I had a dream last night... I'm sure it was just a dream.

Upsy was sitting on the side of my bed, looking at me with such sadness in her eyes, as though she could see my future. She was whole and perfect. She was beautiful, nothing like the bloated, mottled, corpse that haunts my nightmares. She didn't say anything, she didn't stay long. When I woke up, I was alone.

Later that day, Marva and I are back on the bus to the city. I'm a million miles away, thinking about Upsy, trying to figure out the mystery of her visits. She wants me to run, but from what? What does she want me to see? Is she jealous that I have a new friend now – is she upset because of Marva? I haven't been sleeping well, I'm not myself lately. It's all getting to me. I'm lost in thought when the bus stops.

I've held onto the modelling agency's phone number and address for a long time, clinging to the hope it represents. Life with Mother and Jim is just as unbearable as life with Magda was. I'm 17 years old now and I need to look after myself. I need to move on, and hopefully this is the way to do it. After a quick stop to do some business, we grab a cab and head to the agency. We pull up in front of a multistory, nondescript wood and brick building with no windows. It's not at all what I expected, I anticipated a fancy office in a high-rise building in the centre of the city. I'm disappointed, and my intuition is telling me to turn around and leave.

The cab drives off, leaving us in this dismal, seedy part of town. I look up at the building which sits next door to a fenced off abandoned lot; the overgrown grass speaking to its long-untouched state. Across the street are more tall, nondescript buildings; we are in the industrial area of town, grungy and grimy and eerily quiet. I'm leery, but Marva is excited, like we're on an adventure. Her enthusiasm is contagious, and I let her grab my hand and pull me up the steps, towards the big wooden door. There's no answer when we knock. Marva's sure they can't hear us, so she pushes on the door and it opens enough for us to walk in. We are standing in a large empty space, resembling a warehouse.

Marva is yelling, "Hello?"

A woman appears. She has a long dark hair, bright red lips

and is wearing a tight black dress. She strides towards us on impossibly high black stiletto heels. She certainly looks like a movie star. Maybe this is just a shooting location, maybe everything will be alright. This is my chance and I need to take it, eagerly telling her we're here about the ad. She looks us over, settling on Marva with a disapproving gaze. Marva's long nose, along with her bright orange, frizzy hair and bell bottom jeans were hardly model-worthy, and she knew it. Marva points at me – this isn't her dream, it's mine. The woman nods and looks back at me, nodding approvingly.

As she introduces herself as Ava, she reaches out her hand and runs her fingers through my long, blond hair. I had recently let Marva cut it, parting it in the middle and giving me long sweeping bangs and layers of waves. I was glad I had the foresight to dress better than Marva, wearing tight jeans, with knee high boots and a colourfully floral ruched crop top. I thought I looked good; and I know I'm pretty, at least that's what the guys tell me as they are breathing heavy in my ear.

She leads us upstairs to an open loft where a few more

people are milling around; all turn to look at us. Ava explains that we have come about the ad. A tall man puts down the papers in his hand and walks over to us with a smirk. He's dressed in a suit, no tie, open at the neck revealing a gold necklace. He shakes our hands, holding mine a little longer than necessary. After taking Ava aside to speak with her, he walks away and Ava brings us to a room deep in the back of the building, telling Marva to wait here in the outer part; the waiting room. She opens another door and ushers me in, smiles and closes the door. This room has lighting and a camera set up in front of a bench with a sheet thrown over it. The room is not inviting, rather dark and gloomy. Marva and I are separated. I don't like this, every ounce of me is screaming – but I want this so bad. I want out so bad. I want to believe...

The man with the gold necklace walks in. What happens next, is not what I expected, not what I wanted, and something I will bury so deep that I'll hardly even remember it for the rest of my life. But I will remember the sting, the betrayal, the disappointment...the realization that dreams of fame and fortune will come with a price.

Suffice to say, he starts telling me how to pose, how to move, and snapping pictures all the while, telling me to smile and loosen up, move my hair this way and that. Click, click, click goes the camera, the dim room lighting up with every flash. Then he expects me to take off my clothes. I don't have a lot in life, but my dignity is not for sale...not yet anyway... but I get ahead of myself. When I grab my clothes and try to leave, I find the door is locked. I panic and starting banging on it, yelling for Marva. She starts calling my name and banging on the other side, knowing something is wrong.

I'm begging and pleading to get out when the door opens, and another man comes in the room. He has pushed Marva aside, and I see her getting up off the ground, charging back towards the door. It slams in her face, and he stands between me and the door, blocking it...

Later on, back on the bus, Marva is looking at me with a stricken look on her face, urging me to tell her what happened. I don't speak. How can I tell her what happened in that room? I'm not even sure myself. Hands were all over me, holding me down... the cameraman snapped pictures continuously... the flashes in the dark room are emblazoned on the back of my eyelids. My eyes were closed tight, as if not seeing it happen would make it not real. They got their pictures, they got what they wanted... I don't know where those pictures are going to end up... After a million minutes, the camera stopped whirring and clicking, and it was over...they threw some bills at me and unlocked the door. I wasn't crying, I was numb...I was confused and ashamed. I rushed out of there and didn't stop running until it hit me like a ton of bricks and I sank to the sidewalk, sobbing. Marva is worried that I'm mad at her. Why would I be? It was all own my own dumb fault for thinking an ad stapled to a post was going to make me a star.

I have many regrets in my life, but one of the biggest is that I was never smart enough to trust that little voice in my head. I could have saved myself so much heartache. It's always been there, trying to tell me something, not unlike Upsy, but I became good at ignoring it, much to my own detriment. I have always second guessed myself, leading me, and later others, into some dire circumstances.

The experience in the city was a huge blow to my self esteem, to my dreams, to my hope of a better future. I find myself sinking into a deep depression that I can't seem to shake. Hanging on to my dreams was keeping me alive, keeping me sane...and I feel like I've lost it all. I begin drinking more, caring less...it's a vicious cycle.

Marva tries to rally me, encourage me...but there's a blackness casting a shadow over me that won't leave. Sometimes late at night, before I fall asleep, I talk to Upsy. Even in death, she is the only one I can pour my heart out to. With soft whispers only the dead themselves can hear, I confess all my sins and fears and beg her to help me, send me a sign, just let me know everything is going to be alright. She hasn't visited me in awhile; the nightmares seem to have settled down a bit. I'm left with nothing, no one. There seems to be only one option...

It's almost midnight. I've just left Marva's place, we've been drinking, as always. Alcohol is a depressant, I'm told, and I can certainly feel that...the only thing my beloved escape has provided me with tonight is sadness. I should go back home, but instead I'm just aimlessly walking. I don't want to go home – Jim's place isn't home anyway. Missouri is home, but even there...that wasn't living. I've never been able to find happiness, the elusive reward for all the struggles and strife. What's the point of it all anyway? It all just seems so hopeless.

My mind, as it does when it's quiet, always goes back to Upsy, and I find myself replaying the same script over and over. I just want to go back in time and change everything...back to that day that I left Upsy at the river, after saying the most unforgivable things. She never would have left me alone, like I did to her. She was a better person, a good person... and I was a monster. If only I could apologize, beg her forgiveness... I find myself heading towards the beach at very end of Marva's street. And I continue walking...down the forested path and onto the beach sand. The moon is full and bright, lighting a trail to the water. The beach is empty... I'm all alone. My mind is blank and I don't stop walking. Without any hesitation, I walk right into the water....the cold is a bit of a shock to the system but I don't stop...up to my knees...my clothes are soaked and I start to shiver...up to my hips....the water is starting to slow me down.....up to my neck...the water hits my mouth and I involuntarily swallow a mouthful. I choke and sputter. Then, and only then, do I stop walking. It would be so easy to take one more step, to experience what Upsy felt that day. I imagine her coming up from under the water in front of me and pulling me back under with her. But she's not here – neither to save me, nor to take me with her. This choice is mine alone. The night is still and quiet. My eyes want to close and my legs want to buckle. My body is yearning just to float away, sink below the surface and just wait for whatever the other side holds. But some strength that I don't even realize I have makes me take a step backwards... then another.....

When I finally get home, I'm wet and freezing. No one is awake to see me come in. I peel off my clothes, dry off and climb into bed exhausted, mind blank...having no idea what stopped me.

VIII

I'm sleeping so deeply that I don't hear it at first. My eyes struggle to open. What is that noise? It sounds like a low, deep hum...I listen more closely...no, more like a moan...not a sound of pain, but of sorrow. It's close, but where is it coming from? Down the hall? Is it Mother? Before I can get out of bed to go and check, I catch a movement out of the corner of my eye. A hand is coming up over the side of the bed. Long, grey fingers grab a hold of the top of the mattress, searching... My mouth is open to scream, but I can't breathe. Leaning ever so slightly over the side of the bed, I stretch my neck as far as it will go, struggling to see....In one sudden, disjointed movement, Upsy pulls herself out from under the bed. Her body cracks and bends unnaturally, with exaggerated stiffness, until she is standing upright in front of me. Her brow is deeply furrowed, there's an angry scowl on her pale, lifeless face; the skin peeling away to reveal bone.

Her skeletal hand grabs my arm and pulls me off the bed. In one swift motion, she pushes me into the open closet and slams the door shut. I don't understand what is happening. Sheer terror overcomes me, rendering me frozen in place. All I can do is hunker down in the corner and cover my eyes – I don't want to see anything, I don't want to know what's happening right now. The silence is deafening, as if the darkness itself is speaking to me. I can feel Upsy standing behind me, not moving; her raspy, ragged voice whispers at the back of my ear, "Open your eyes..." When I do, I'm no longer in the closet, I'm standing in the garage, my bare toes curl trying to get away from the cold, hard floor. I begin to shake, looking all over...he's here somewhere, I can feel him. The garage smells strongly of motor oil and cigarettes; a smell so familiar...I wrinkle my nose.

Beside me, the garage door opens. A little girl walks in, carrying an open bottle of beer. Her hair hides her face, only the tip of a small nose peeks out from behind. Carefully and slowly, she walks past Upsy and I, trying not to spill a drop. Her little summer sun dress swings around her knees as she moves. She's walking towards a car that's been jacked up – then I notice legs underneath – someone is lying under there. Clanking and banging tools...fixing something...changing oil... She stands quietly until he notices her, grabbing her bare feet playfully from under the car. She squeals in delight; a drop of beer spilling on the ground. He begins to push himself out from under the car...inch by inch his body slides out...it's not a dark figure...it's a man...his features are clear... I see him...

I slam my eyes shut, moaning no... no...no... Upsy pulls my hands away from my face, "Look!" She commands.

I'm shuddering and sobbing, every ounce of my being in resisting, but Upsy's will is too strong. I open my eyes...

Uncle Mink is standing in front of the little girl, a cigarette hanging out the corner of his mouth. He throws it on the ground and crushes it beneath his feet. Then he accepts the beer, sitting cross legged on the floor beside the car, inviting her to do the same. Her back is to me, I don't know who she is. I can only see her long hair. Upsy? Is that you?

They sit on the floor laughing and giggling – I can't hear what they're saying. He drinks his beer in a few big gulps and throws the bottle into the backseat of the car, into a pile of at least half a dozen others, half covered by a grey wool blanket. A half empty liquor bottle also sits on the floor. He's been drinking all afternoon, one after another. His words are slurred, his movements are slow and clumsy. He starts tickling her, she's giggling and squirming. He pulls her down to the ground, still tickling her, holding her there. She's not laughing anymore; she wants up but he won't let her go. He's not tickling anymore...what is he doing...I can't see... I don't want to see...She's wriggling underneath him, trying to get away...he's got his head resting in the crook of her neck, talking softly...reassuring her.. calming her...hurting her. He doesn't stop, despite her pleas. She's crying softly...she doesn't understand...

I put my hands over my face, collapsing to the ground.

Upsy sits down beside me and pulls my hands away from my eyes, "Watch!" she says softly, pleading with me to understand...

The garage door opens again beside us. Mother walks in...wiping her hands on the apron she's wearing over her summery dress. I look up at her, her wedge heeled sandals make her look so tall. Her blood red toenails are the only colour I can see. Everything is unfolding in shades of grey... in slow motion...I can't stop it.

She sees Uncle Mink and what he's doing. There's no mistaking what is happening in that garage. I can't make out the expression on her face. He notices her and quickly grabs the blanket from the back seat and throws it haphazardly over the little girl, covering her exposed skin. Time is frozen...it seems like minutes pass in that single moment. She says something to him, turns around shaking her head and walks out again. Help her, I scream! Don't leave! What are you doing? Don't leave her there! Don't leave me there! Me...

The little girl turns her head and looks right at us. It's me... it's me... she left me there...with him...

And that's how I died when I was five.

Not physically, but something deep inside me died...my soul, my spirit...a small flame snuffed out. Everything went black...and I learned how to float away, to separate from myself and my memories – to protect that little girl. No one else protected her, so her own mind did; fractured in a million pieces and changed who she would be...and how she would be. And it was all buried deep in my heart, remaining a mystery until this very moment.

I'm back in my bed gasping and sobbing, Upsy sits beside me silently. The cloak of death is gone and she's beautiful and whole again. I believe her, everything she said that Uncle Mink did to her... I knew it was true all along... I just didn't want to believe it... or I would be forced to come face to face with my own hurt and trauma. I wasn't ready, I couldn't do it...it was easier to blame her, accuse her... She was trying to get me to see what was right in front of me all along. Everyone knew, except me....

She seems to understand all the thoughts in my head... she knows I'm sorry...everything is alright now. She puts a hand on my shoulder and smiles. She whispers, "Now run." And I know what she means. I know it's time to go. There is nothing, and no one, for me here.

Years of Redemption

I

In the light of day, everything is so clear. The revelation
of the night before hangs heavy in my mind, but a fog has
lifted and now I see everything for what it is...and
everyone for who they are. It explains so much...so much
about me is tied up in the past, caused by the past. I don't
know why it took me so long to understand, but my eyes
are wide open. I have Upsy to thank for that. Knowing she
forgives me and she'll always be watching over me, is the
only thing that is keeping me sane right now.

I need to get out of this house, in order to deal with
everything and everyone. I feel like I'm on the verge of
self-destructing and I'm afraid of what I might do. I don't
know how to deal with this, but I do know one thing, I'm
finally able to take Upsy's advice. I'm ready to run.

I'm up and out of the house before anyone else is awake.
Seeing as how neither of them work, Mother and Jim tend
to stay up late and sleep until noon. I can't see her right
now...I wouldn't handle it well. I need to clear my head. I

need time to think.

I turned 18 last week; I'm officially an adult. But today, I feel like a broken child who needs comfort and someone to tell her everything will be alright. There's a tender wound deep in my heart that may never heal properly. My body no longer feels like my own. I don't know myself...I don't know anything anymore... For the first time since he left, I really want to talk to Freddie. I feel all alone in the world right now and I need my brother. We weren't terribly close growing up, but he's the only one that would understand all the history, the backstory, the relationships involved in this mess of a life. I want him to know. I want to know if he knew all along. I need to reconnect with him. I've memorized the phone number he left me; it's seared into the back of my mind. and I try calling again, but not surprisingly there is no answer.

I have a list of things I need to do before I can go. I head to Marva's to clear my head. She's home alone, as usual. Her father is always working or sleeping. He doesn't realize that he's losing her slowly. He's going to wake up one day and find that she resents him, and no longer needs him at all. Leaving her to her own devices this long, and not helping her heal from her mother's death is going to fracture their relationship for good. She's not going to be the same person she would have been if she had his support and attention. It's so easy to be on the outside looking in – so easy to see what other people need to do in their lives. But in my own situation, everything is murky and I don't know which way to turn.

We spend the day together and I pour out my heart to her. I've never told Marva that Upsy has been haunting me, and I won't share that with her now. I don't think Upsy will scare me anymore, but I do hope she visits from time to time. Marva knows I've been plagued by bad dreams, but I've never really explained them. I never really talked about them at all since my days of talking to Mrs. Delaney. Ever since then, I've kept them to myself. They were always my burden to hold. Now I know they were given to me; gifted by an evil man and his sister who condoned it all. But today, I need to talk. I need to get all the garbage out of my head to clear the slate and make room for new adventures.

So we spend the day curled up on her couch, drinking and talking. And as the alcohol relaxes me, I'm able to tell her the words I didn't think I would ever be able to say out loud. I need to say them, so I can say them again later when I confront the woman who caused all my pain. She cries with me, holds my hand, and provides silent support as I spill my guts all over the room. For all that I tell her, I don't mention Upsy, and the horrible fate she came to because of me. That is my own personal shame and I will carry that cross for the rest of my life. I speak the rest of my truth, until the tears stop. It's been an emotional day, and to break the tension and sombreness, we order a pizza. She wants to invite the gang over and have a party, but I say no. I just need for it to be her and I, just this one last time. Besides, I need to sober up, clear my head and be in control when I return home.

It's getting late, I need to move on to the rest of my plan. So, at the end of the evening, I'm standing on Marva's front porch, taking a moment longer to stay goodbye. She's in a good mood when I leave; she's always laughing and smiling. It hides her pain, I know this, but I never let on, because I don't want to be the one to break her dam.

We all have our lot in life, our struggles and trials, and this is how she copes. Far be it for me to take this away from her. I turn to leave, but then turn back and give her a long hug, whispering, "Thank you," in her ear. She's taken aback; a little surprised. I've never hugged her before. But she leans in to the hug and I memorize everything about her. She doesn't know that I'm leaving. She doesn't know that she won't see me again until decades have passed. There's no need to tell her. Her life will also take twists and turns. She will move away and we will eventually come together again, however briefly.

I walk home under the dull streetlights, along the quiet road. The warm breeze blows through my hair, as I kick a rock in front of me absent-mindedly. A few cars drive by, a couple walking their dog pass me, but otherwise, it's just me and my thoughts. I know what I need to do. I'm afraid to do it, but I can't move forward unless I face my fears. I need to do this alone. I don't have much strength or will left after living the life I have. The recent discovery about my past and the recovered memories have devastated me to the core, but I'm going to need to scrape together every ounce of strength I can muster to get through this next chapter of my life. I feel all alone in the world, but then again, I always have been. This is a battle I need to fight myself.

Approaching the house, the lights are still on and Jim's truck is gone. He's probably at his weekly bowling game, which usually ends up at the bar. Mother never goes with him, she'll be home alone. I don't know if she really loves Jim; it is his lifestyle she really coveted. She's willing to put up with him if it means she never has to see herself as poor again. He's a causality in her plan, irrelevant really...but then again, maybe he sees her that way too. Maybe he's settling for her also, to have someone, anyone to grow old with, to look after him and the house. What a complicated and tangled web our lives are. Does anyone ever get it right? Or does everyone have to make allowances? I am determined to create the life I want...to be so far removed from the life I've lived. In order to do that I need money, and small time drug dealing isn't going to cut it. My fortune awaits me, I just have to get there. And the plan begins tonight.

I open the door quietly and walk in the house. Mother is

sitting in front of the television, drink in hand, and acknowledges me only with a side glance. She hasn't cared about my comings and goings for some time, so I'm not worried about being blindsided when I'm not ready. I head up to my room, close and lock the door. I take out a large duffle bag from my closet and look around the room. I don't know where to start, but I soon realize that I'm going to be leaving most of my stuff behind. And that's alright, I don't have much attachment to anything anyway. I have no sentimental items really, save for the necklace that Mrs. Delaney gave me, the bracelet I made for Upsy, and the note Freddie left for me the night he too, ran away from this life. I pack as many clothes and shoes as I can, plus jewellery, makeup, and the small box containing my treasures. I put the roll of money I've been saving in the inside pocket of my jean jacket, vowing to find a safer place later. It's not a lot of money, but it's a enough to get me away, so I can start over again.

Then it's time. I leave the bedroom without looking back, and head down the stairs. Mother is still watching television, still drinking, and doesn't turn her head. I walk forward and stand in the living room doorway until she notices me.

"Where are you going with that big bag packed at this hour? You spend so much time with that Marva girl, you might as well just go live there." She makes a 'hmph' noise and turns back to her television show, draining the rest of her drink. The ice cubes tinkle in her glass, bringing me right back to the old house in Missouri, where she refilled that glass and those ice cubes all day long, becoming more and more mean as the day went on. The tinkling of ice will forever remind me of my mother.

I set my bag behind me, in the hall, in front of the door. Then I walk further into the room. She's ignoring me, probably wishing I would go away. She'll get her wish soon enough, but after I've had my say. I go to the television and turn it off, standing in front of it. I expect this to elicit some sort of reaction, but it doesn't. She merely sighs, setting her glass down and looking up at me, waiting.

"I'm leaving." I say simply.

She shrugs, telling me to move out of the way of the television, and that she won't be leaving the door unlocked for me when I get back.

She's not getting it. I tell her that I've packed a bag; I'm leaving and won't be coming back.

She snorts derisively, "Ok, I'll play along. Where are you going?"

Her dismissive manner causes something inside me to break. All the anger that I've been harbouring throughout the years, all the pain from the recently recovered memories, all the rage from years of neglect and abuse, all come flooding to the surface before I can even begin to control them.

I scream at her then. When I was younger, under her control, I had no voice. I have found my voice now. I tell her what a horrible mother she was my whole life, that Freddie left because of how she treated us, and let the men in her life treat us. And now she is losing me too. Even though I am strong, I am still fearful of her possible reaction. Never once did I ever go against her like this. She never expected this from me, and at first she doesn't know how to react.

What she does do, is pick up her glass, get up and go across the room to the little bar cart in the corner and big to fix herself another drink, and as she does that she begins to speak.

"Do you think it's easy to raise children, Annie?" She doesn't look at me, as she puts more ice in her glass. Tinkle, tinkle...the sound makes me cringe. When I don't reply, she continues, "Do you think it's easy to raise children with no family support or help, with no money. You have no idea what my life was like, and trying to raise two children...two ungrateful troublemakers...who were always underfoot and were never....." She stops, not finishing her sentence. But I knew that last word was going to be "wanted". She didn't have to say it. She made us feel it every day. This only fuels my anger, and I lash out.

"Three children, Mother. Three. Pearly-May was your

child too!"

No one had spoken the baby's name for the past 15 years. Pearly-May would be 15 years old now. Someone had to speak for her.

The shock on her face is satisfying. She takes a long drink, then slams the glass down and turns towards me. But before she can speak, I continue, "You think I don't know...I know everything! I may have been little, but I was in your room that night and I saw you lying on top of her. I remember all of it. You were drunk and passed out...and you killed her!" I raged. I was shaking and sweating, as though the memories were purging themselves through my skin.

She yells over top of me, calling me stupid and delusional, saying that I don't have a clue what I'm talking about. She says that I better never breathe a word of these lies to anyone else, or I'll be sorry. And I know in that moment, her greatest concern isn't me telling the police, it's me telling Jim. If he found out, it might be distasteful, even to him, and she might lose her comfortable lifestyle and end up at the bottom of the barrel again. Only this time, she'll be all alone...and fending for herself is a fate worse than jail.

When she finishes, she puts a hand to her chest, catching her breath. This is affecting her, taking a lot of her. It's satisfying... and I continue.

I growl at her, telling her how disgusting it was that she was angry at me for Cleve paying attention to me. I was just a little girl, and she treated me like her competition for a man that was no prize. She shakes her head, and with a wave of her hand, tries dismissing my claims. When I ask her if she knew he was sneaking in my room at night, the blood draining from her face tells me she, in fact, did not. She looks devastated, still pining for Cleve, who left her voluntarily...no man had ever left her voluntarily and it had hurt her deeply. It still seems it hurt her even more to know that Cleve was more interested in her daughter, than herself. She calls me a dirty liar, in a low voice, riddled with doubt, confusion and pain. I'm breaking her...she's not a strong woman, she never has been. This confrontation will fill her with self doubt, age her, and if nothing else, fill her with shame.

In fact, I make sure to let her know how ashamed she should be at the way she treated her children – the physical abuse, emotional abuse – always yelling at us, hitting us and making us feel worthless. And the drinking...always drinking...just a drunk.

Her anger rears its ugly head then, and she reverts back to something I didn't expect, when she screams at me, "Blows that wound cleans away evil; strokes make clean the inner most parts! Proverbs 20:30 say so!"

I am incredulous, "Are you trying to justify all the abuse with your Bible verses? Do you expect me to believe that you hit us and hurt us to clean away our evil? To make us better people?" I laugh, and look away, shaking my head. "There is no justification for what you put us through. You weren't saving our souls, you just didn't care, you never wanted us, you never loved us!"

She doesn't deny it, but she shakes her head ruefully and sits down on the couch, hands clasped between her knees.

She's worn out, she has no good arguments for her behaviour. She doesn't have a leg to stand on right now.

There's one thing left to say.

"I remember about Uncle Mink...when I was five."

She looks up at me wide-eyed, her jaw drops. Her mouth is open, but she's unable to make a sound.

That's right, I say, I remember it all - the smell of the cigarette smoke and motor oil; the feeling of the cold, hard garage floor on my back; the rough grey wool blanket hastily thrown over me; the smell of Uncle Mink's cologne, and the weight of his body. And I remember her...how she came in then, in her summer dress and wedge heeled sandals, and blood red toenails...the only colour I could see in that garage and then forevermore in my dreams. She found us, saw what he was doing, saw where his hands were. She said something, I don't know what, the blood rushing through my ears blocked out the sound. Then she turned around and left. She left me alone with a monster, and that monster would haunt my sleep for years to come. But not anymore; I don't have any bad dreams anymore.

She mumbled something...I couldn't believe my ears.

"What did you just say?!" My heart breaks in a million pieces.

"I told him it was time to come in for supper."

I can hear the garage door slam, as she left that day.

He was unsure, he wasn't expecting that reaction - no reaction. And I remember the rest of it. His tool box fell over when he kicked it as he jumped up, adjusting his clothes and rushing out after her. He had to know whether she was going to call the police, or what he could do to ensure she didn't. He left me lying there, broken and damaged. Forever changed in ways I'd never understand. The only way I would be able to get through it all, was to forget it, bury it, deny it...until it existed only in the very depths of my subconscious. I had developed a hard shell, built a thick wall, and created armour to protect myself from all of it. It kept trying to creep back through the cracks as I slept, but it wasn't until Upsy forced me to see, that I was able to remember. A piece of me was left behind in that garage, and that's why I could never go back in. That poor little girl is still alone in there.

Mother is hanging her head, perhaps in shame, it doesn't matter anymore. I got it all off my chest, out of my head and now I am spent. It's time to go.

"Where are you going to go?" She wants to know, looking up at me.

She doesn't deserve to know, and while I debate whether or not to tell her, headlights shine in the window and a truck pulls in the driveway. Jim is home.

When he opens the door and sees us both, and my bag on the floor, he knows he has just walked in on something. The tension in the room is unmistakable. The angry words and forgotten memories linger like plumes of smoke, poisoning the air, making it hard to breathe.

"What's going on?" he bellows, throwing his keys on the little table by the door and putting his hands on his hips.

Mother is visibly happy to see him, perking up considerably. She stands up, as he walks over to her. He knows he should be angry, and he's waiting to find out why.

"Annie says she's leaving, and she's not coming back." Her voice has no emotion in it.

"Oh really?" He turns back to me, "And just where might you be going at midnight?"

He's smirking at me. And Mother is pulling strength from Jim's presence, becoming her old self, her anger returning. She truly is nothing without a man. They both stand stoic, looking at me, waiting for me to speak.

When I tell them that I am going to California to be a model, or an actress and I won't be coming back, they look at each other and begin to laugh. Condescension oozes from their faces and lips as they proceed to tell me what a foolish girl I am, what a stupid idea my dream is... that I have no hope in Hell of becoming famous, and surely not as a model. They take turns brow beating and berating me. They patronize me, mock me, and stomp all over the hope that I've been holding onto since I was a little girl. I'm not tall enough, not skinny enough, not good enough... It's all a big joke to them.

But I was prepared for this reaction. The only reason that I didn't leave in the middle of the night without telling her, is because I needed to have this confrontation with Mother. I needed her to know that I'm not a child anymore, and she can no longer keep me under the heel of her boot; she can no longer control me. But most of all, despite all the abuse and neglect, I *will* succeed in life. The satisfaction of throwing in her face everything I know and remember was worth it. She's acting like she doesn't care right now, but if she has any shred of humanity, she will have to come to terms with the fact that she has pushed away both her children. When she is alone, in her quiet moments, she will realize that she hurt us both to the point where we no longer care about her. Then she will realize how truly alone in the world she is.

They are still laughing, as I pick up my bag and walk out the door. I look back over my shoulder to see them waving gleefully through the window. They think I will fail; they are sure I will return with my tail between my legs. They are looking forward to holding my failure over my head for the rest of my life. But I won't let that happen. I'm determined to prove them wrong and wipe the smile of their faces. I'd rather kill myself than come back here.

II

By the time I get to the bus station, it's almost two a.m. The station is quiet, save for a couple travellers and a few homeless people using the station to stay off the streets. I purchase a ticket, which takes up more of my money than I was expecting, but I'll still be alright. I just need to get to California and then I can make good things start happening.

As I wait for the next bus to arrive, which isn't for another couple hours, I plan what I need to do. As soon as I get there, I need to find a place to stay, that should be fairly easy; any cheap motel will do. The next thing I have to do is find a job, any job, and I need to find one fast. But before I can even let myself think too much about the happiness that awaits me, there are a couple other things I need to take care of.

I'm deep in thought when the bus arrives. I take a window seat near the back and settle in. As it pulls away from the station, leaving this little North Carolina town behind, the air is suddenly different – it's as though I've been holding my breath for the last 18 years. For the first time, I can breathe... I inhale deep and long, and my mind is free. I can feel the difference. And that's when I know, I'm doing the right thing. I have to believe that all the trouble and strife I've been through was all worth it and will amount to something in the end, because if it doesn't, what was the point of it all? If I can't rise above, I think I will just die inside. If this doesn't work, I can't fathom what the rest of my life will be like. My journey was long and hard, but I can finally see a light at the end of the tunnel.

The bus heads West, seemingly at a crawl; the hours are

long and there's nothing to do except stare out the window into the night. Miles go on and on. Different people get on and off at every stop, but I remain in my seat, watching them come and go. I wonder what their lives are like, what they are running from, or maybe to. Old, young, men, women; they all have a story. I wonder if any of them have a story like mine. Surely the world can't be that sad. A little girl boarding the bus catches my eye. She's wearing a pretty dress covered by a small knitted sweater. She must only be 3 or 4 years old, and she's struggling to climb up the bus steps; her hand being held by her mother. She reminds me of Upsy, of myself. The top step is too high for her little legs. I smile when her mother picks her up, carrying her on her hip, and kisses her on the cheek before setting her down on the big bench seat. It makes me happy, yet sad at the same time. Didn't I deserve that too? Why did little Annie never get a kiss on the cheek, or the feeling of love and security? Little bubbles of anger begin to rise to the surface, and I look away from the little girl and her mother...leaving them to a world that I have never experienced. It just doesn't matter anymore.

The further I get away from North Carolina, the more I

reminisce about my life, my past, my childhood. There
were good times – time spent with Upsy and Mrs. Delaney
bring a small smile to my face. I'm doing this for them, as
much as myself. I'll succeed for them. I won't let my
impoverished, volatile childhood crush my will or my
spirit. If nothing else, I've developed strength,
independence and the ability to take care of myself. But a
tough outer shell hides a tortured soul.

I'm dozing, slouched in the seat; the hood of the sweatshirt
that I'm wearing under my jean jacket is half covering my
face, when the bus pulls into yet another station. We have
crossed into Tennessee. Now it's time for me to move. I
follow the line of people off the bus, as though I'm in a
herd of cattle. I'm impatient, and even though I know it's a
ridiculous notion, as soon as I step foot on the ground I
find myself looking around at all the faces, looking for
Freddie. I'm hoping against hope that by some miracle he
happens to be nearby. I know realistically that Tennessee
is a big state, but I'm closer to him now than I've been in
many years. He seems to be so close, yet so far. I need to
find him, to see his familiar face – my enemy in childhood
could now be my best friend. I just need him, or someone,

anyone, to tell me that everything is going to be alright. So much has happened since he left. Part of me is afraid that he's forgotten about me. I push through the crowd and head straight for the pay phone. I want to hear his voice so badly that I say a little prayer as I drop my quarter into the slot. As usual, it rings and rings.... I let it ring a million times before I hang up.

III

The next step in my plan is monumental. Having failed to reach Freddie, I have to abandon that for now, stop dwelling on it and focus on my next goal. I'm nervous, but determined. I change buses, altering my route to California slightly. There's two more things I need to do – two more doors that need to be closed. One joyous, the other terrifying, but so cathartic.

Leaving Tennessee with sadness in my heart, the bus makes its way into Missouri. As soon as we cross State lines, I can feel it - the pull of home, the ghosts of the past... The next hours on the bus, in that small, cramped space feel like an eternity. I play out scenes in my mind, scripting how I want things to happen, how it will all unfold, so I'm prepared...but ultimately return to all the what ifs and the trepidation. A moment of anxiety brings with it a silent panic attack, causing me to question what I'm even doing, who do I think I am, what right do I have...Will I be strong enough to do what I need to do while I'm here? The thought of leaving the familiarity of Missouri and moving on to the unknown of California causes a new wave a fear. The negative voices in my head echo Mother's words back to me – I'm not good enough or pretty enough, I'll never make it. Do I have the strength to do any of this, or should I just turn around and go home with my tail between my legs? The miles pass, as I sit and stare straight ahead, appearing calm to anyone who may glance over at me, but inside my mind is churning and my stomach is in knots.

The bus passes by the turn leading into my hometown. I watch it pass, knowing I'll be back soon. I need to get something else out of the way first, before I can go home. We travel on another couple hours, before stopping at a larger city that I had never been to in my life, even though we lived close by. Oh, I had the opportunity to go into the city once, but I refused... and Mother had gone alone. She went to visit Uncle Mink alone that day. Today, I'm going alone also.

Walking away from the busy bus station, I don't know where exactly I'm going, but I'll find my way. I end up needing to get a taxi to bring me to the prison which was just outside town. I had planned for this expense, I still have enough money. I could have saved money not taking this side trip, but I think I need to do this. I need to confront Uncle Mink like I confronted Mother. It will be so empowering; offering me closure. Most importantly, he'll know that he didn't get away with it. It's not a secret buried deep in my heart anymore. I'll be giving him back the shame he bestowed on me.

I ask the taxi to wait, and leave my bag in the backseat. I don't plan for this to take long. We are not going to have a happy reunion; we aren't going to have lots to talk about. I'm going to sting him with what I have to say, with all the words that I have planned since that night I remembered everything. Then, I'm going to turn my back on him and walk away, after giving him a look of disgust and pity. I'll leave him behind, trapped in the prison of his own doing, just like he left me alone in the garage after destroying the little girl I was. He'll feel small and disgraced, just like I did. That is the only revenge I can have at this point, but it's a small victory nonetheless.

I walk nervously inside the imposing brick building, the back of which is surrounded by barbed wire, to keep in all the evil that lies within its walls. People in uniforms are milling around as I try to get my bearings and figure out where to start. I can't just tell them I'm here to confront a horrible, horrible man. They won't care – there are many horrible men here. I need to follow my plan, to stare him in the eye, face to face, and have my say.

Approaching the large desk, an older woman with large glasses smiles kindly and asks how she can help me. I need to find out what time visiting hours are, and get myself put on the visitor's list. The secretary confirms it is visiting hours, but says I may have to come back another time if I'm a new visitor. They need to get the inmate's permission to put me on the visitor list. I know he'll add me, I can wait one more day if I have to. She asks me who I wish to see, and I say, "Byron Minkus". She pulls out a large black binder, and tucks her hair behind her ear as she leafs through, turning to the M's. She purses her lips in concentration, as she follows the list down with her finger, once, then twice.

She closes the binder and looks up at me, with a look on her face that I can't read, "No worries, I have another book."

She pulls a blue binder off the shelf and flips to the M's once again. Slowly she goes over each name on the list. From where I'm standing, I see his name myself, written in block letters.

"There it is!" I point it out, as her finger lands on it at the same time.

She closes the book and sighs, giving me a soft smile.

"I'm sorry," she says, "Byron Minkus is no longer in this prison."

I'm a bit surprised. Was he released, or transferred? How will I ever find him now? I don't have enough money to travel to another prison; he might have even been sent to another state.

Before I can ask any questions, she says, "I'm sorry to be the one to tell you, but Byron Minkus died in prison last year."

I take a step back, shock reverberating through my body. I wasn't expecting this. It never struck me that he might not be here, that I wouldn't get to confront him and do what I need to do to heal my soul. I slump against the desk, tears falling, as I cry quietly. All the adrenaline that I've been carrying since the bus arrived in Missouri leaves my body in a rush. The despair I'm feeling weighs me down heavily, as though I'm carrying the world on my shoulders. How will I ever mend my heart? In the end, he's robbed me for a second time; not of my innocence this time, but of my hope, my closure.

The sympathetic secretary is sorry she's upset me; sorry that she had to deliver the news that I obviously hadn't known. She looks in the book again, and tells me there's a notation that they had tried to contact family, but the number given for next of kin was out of service. Of course, it was – because Mother had lost the house and we had moved long before. I thank the woman for her help and she pats me on the hand with a smile, before turning back to her work.

I'm gutted as I walk back outside and get in the taxi. All the feelings I had after that last nightmare...after I finally remembered...are mixing with new feelings of anger, of mourning the loss of myself... and the inability to recover myself. I'm so mad at Uncle Mink; he has stolen so much from me. As a child, he robbed me of my purity and my memory, splitting me into two separate souls – one forever in the dark, and the other who will always be searching for the light. And now, as an adult, he's robbed me of the confrontation that would reunite the two. I will always be fractured; I won't ever be whole...and being aware of it all ensures that I will spend the rest of my life looking for something to fill the void.

The taxi takes me back to the bus station. I still have more to do.

IV

I get off the bus at the station in the little town where I used to live. A long time has passed, but nothing has changed, as though it has been frozen in time, waiting for me to come back. The town is small; I'm able to walk wherever I need to go. My bag is heavy, but manageable, and I hoist it over my shoulder and begin to walk out of town towards my old house. I just need to see it, maybe knock on the door and ask if I can go in and look around. And on the way, I'll stop at Mrs. Delaney's house and hope she's still there. When she answers the door, I'll throw my arms around her and let her know I'm alright, I've survived. I smile, thinking of our reunion and how sweet it will be.

No one really pays attention to me as I'm walking; no one seems to recognize me. It's alright, our family wasn't really well-liked and didn't have many friends. I don't expect to see anyone who would bother talking to me. It isn't a long walk from town to the gravel road leading to my old house. It's a walk I've done a million times, and the familiarity comes rushing back. Every dip in the road, grove of trees, patches of wildflowers and rock formations all in the exact same spot; a map leading me home.

The country road is dotted with houses on either side, which I largely ignore as I walk past. However, when I reach Upsy's old house, I'm torn between going to the door to see if her family still lives there and closing my eyes and walking past. I pause for a moment at the end of the driveway. The large farmhouse stands as a memorial to Upsy – to our time together. It is a marker of her existence, of our childhood, and a reminder that nothing will ever be the same again. In the end, I turn away and continue on. I just can't face her mother, her siblings...I still feel responsible for her death.

Another 649 steps brings me to Mrs. Delaney's house. I hesitate only a moment before starting down the long unpaved driveway to her front porch. After a few tentative steps, I find myself running, suddenly wanting to get there as fast as I can. I knock on the door, excitement building – I just want to see her, hug her, hear her voice again. After a moment a middle aged woman answers the door, wiping her hands on a dish towel. The smell of apple pie follows her.

"Can I help you?" She asks with a smile, but looking at me quizzically. Strangers never show up at your door unexpectedly in these parts.

"Oh..," I'm a little confused, but I find my voice, "I'm looking for Mrs. Delaney?" I look past the woman, into the house.

"Well I'm Mrs. Delaney, but I expect you're looking for my mother in law? Celia Delaney?"

I nod.

"Well, I'm sorry to say she no longer lives here. She's been in the nursing home in town for about a year now. She's had some medical issues and couldn't live on her own anymore. Her youngest son, my husband, took over the house and we moved in...to keep it in the family, you see."

I nod again, words fail me. I never expected her not to be here. But she's still alive, so I will be making an extra stop on my trip before I leave.

"Who did you say you were again?" The other Mrs. Delaney looks at me, waiting for a reply.

I shake my head, with a rueful smile and start to back away, "Just a ghost from the past. Thank you for your help. I might go visit her before I leave town.

"Well, I'm sure she'd like that. She doesn't get many visitors. You take care now." She smiles and closes the door.

Continuing on my way, I focus now on the last 877 steps that it will take to get to my old house from Mrs. Delaney's. I've walked this route so many times over the years that I'm surprised I haven't worn a groove in the road. The air is still, not even a breeze, and the road is quiet. The only sound is that of my feet scuffing along the gravel. With each step I take, I feel like I'm going further and further back in time. I don't know what I'm going to do when I get to the house. Maybe I'll knock on the door and ask if I can come in and look around, or maybe I'll just take a look at my past from the road and quickly walk away. Whatever is going to happen, I have to let it play out. I wonder about the family that lives there now. What will they be like? Are they happy? Do they have a little girl? I hope they are good people. That house deserves a cleansing, some happiness and laughter to soak into its walls to wash away the pain of our years.

And then I see it, emerging slowly around the bend - as though it's moving towards me, instead of me walking towards it. The rundown whitewashed farmhouse sits in the clearing, waiting silently, beckoning me in. A shudder runs through me; a cold lightening bolt from head to toe. Part of me wants to turn and run away, but the other part of me knows that I'll likely never get this opportunity again. I walk down the long driveway to the door, slowly, hesitantly. I expect someone to look out the window, maybe open the door and ask what I'm doing here. I search my mind for an answer, but the closer I get, I soon realize the house is empty. There are no curtains in the windows. It's falling into a state of disrepair. It's been abandoned for awhile, likely since we left. The Sheriff's eviction notice is still pinned to the door, now tattered and crumpled.

I set my bag down on the ground and tentatively walk up the front steps. The long porch runs the length of the house and I can picture Freddie and I there, playing jacks when we were getting along, and fighting when we were weren't. I turn my back to the front door and look around the yard, seeing Rex lumbering in from the barn, and Mother hanging clothes on the line. I never really left; the past is vivid and visceral.

Turning back to the house, I try the front door. Of course it's locked, so I look through the big front window, holding my hand over my eyes, shading the sun. The living room is totally bare – someone had gotten rid of all our belongings – they probably ended up in the dump. Being empty, the room looks much smaller than I remember it to be. It's hard to imagine how all our stuff fit in there.

After a moment, I head around to the back of the house, now overgrown with tall grass and weeds. Below the wooden stairs on the back deck, there is a small window which never did close properly. It slides open easily and I get down on the ground and slip through, landing with a thump on the grungy basement floor. I never did like the basement, filled with cobwebs and gloom, so I quickly head up the steep stairs to the kitchen. I don't want to stay very long because I don't want to get caught, nor do I want to postpone my travels any longer than necessary. But I feel obligated, even compelled, to walk through the house; to validate my childhood.

Moving from room to room on the first floor, I know exactly where everything was - where all the furniture had been...every picture that had been hung, which are now outlines on the grimy walls... where Mother would sit at the kitchen table, drink in hand...Rex slumped on the couch...Freddie and I on the floor in front of the television...

I find myself smiling, purely from nostalgia, as there was nothing good here.

Then I head upstairs to the room that had been my

sanctuary and my prison for many years. Along the way, I pass Mother's room, where Pearly-May died. I say a prayer for the little spirit that remains there, never having had a chance. My bedroom door has been left almost closed, but not shut tight. For some reason, I hesitate for just a moment before I push it open. It's small and dark, with the shadows of the past trapped in the stale air. This is where memories of Cleve appear. I see him smirking, his face right above mine. The memories turn unspeakable, and I shake my head free of them quickly. On the windowsill sits a single black magic marker, maybe it was mine, maybe it belonged to whoever had moved the furniture. I pick it up and take the cap off. On the white painted wall, I write in large letters, "I WAS HERE!" I could have filled the whole wall with my story. Maybe I'll write it all down one day...

It's time to go and I head downstairs, avoiding the creaky third step out of habit. I leave out the front door, well aware that I've left the basement window open a crack. That's alright, it's time the elements get in and take over, destroying the hurt this house holds. If I had a match, I'd burn it to the ground myself.

Back outside now, there's only one thing left to do. I don't want to, but I think I have to - one last confrontation. I head towards the old garage. As I walk towards it, it feels like it's growing, getting bigger and more imposing, as if trying to scare me away...as if daring me to come inside. I haven't set foot in this garage since I was five, except for in my dreams when I always ended up here. My subconscious kept me away, sheltering me from the memories that lie within, saving me from a shock too great to bear. I place my hand on the big wooden door, almost expecting it to burn me, and pull it open.

The dark rushes out at me. I can't see for a moment, so I close my eyes until they adjust. The smell of motor oil is still strong, years worth soaked into the ground like blood, and for just a second, I can't tell the difference between reality and nightmare. Breathing slowly and deeply, I am barely able to get a hold of myself before a full blown panic attack happens. I'm shaking involuntarily, silent tears fill my eyes, threatening to spill. This is where I envision Uncle Mink – I can see him clearly in my mind now – as though his spirit was forced to return here after he died in jail. His sins have tied him to this place, where he will now spend eternity, alone and frightened, just like I was that day.

That thought makes me contented; a small bit of justice that eases my troubled mind. I can leave him here, but I need to free someone else. Little Annie has been trapped here for so long...still laying on the ground, covered with that grey blanket, waiting for someone to save her. I imagine her looking up at me, eyes wide with fear and confusion. She's been waiting a long time...but she's okay...she'll be fine. She'll heal and grow up strong, and build a wall so thick around herself that no one will ever hurt her again. No one will ever get close enough to affect her again. She'll bury it all deep down, until she is numb...but she'll be safe. I'll take care of her, almost like she's my own child – and she'll be the only one I'll ever have space for in my heart. There's no room for anyone else there.

I imagine little Annie getting up off the floor, her summer dress pristine, clean, untouched... A smile slowly develops on her face, her eyes light up. She runs past me out the door, free, liberated...her confinement over. All she needed was someone to open the door. She runs until she fades away in my mind. Maybe she'll find Upsy – that makes me smile. Upsy will take care of little Annie. I turn and walk out of the garage, shutting the door, leaving Uncle Mink behind.

V

I'm feeling calm as I head to the only nursing home in town. A million tons of weight have been lifted off my shoulders. I left a lot of baggage back at that house. I'll never be normal, I've been forever changed by all of it...all the people and events of my past. But there's hope – life is going forward now and I refuse to be stuck in the past any longer.

The nursing home is on the edge of town on a private lot, set in a well landscaped area full of flower beds and benches to sit outside and admire them. It is a one story brick building with the reception area in the middle and the resident's rooms branching out in hallways on both sides. I smile at the elderly lady who sits in a wheelchair near the door, enjoying the sun. She smiles back at me, nodding her head. I hope Mrs. Delaney is happy here. I hope her family visits her often and makes her feel loved and not forgotten. I know what it's like to be forgotten – it's worse for children and older people. We need to feel connected and cherished, because it can sure change you if you aren't.

At the front desk, I ask the young girl where I might find Mrs. Delaney, and she points down the hall on the right, two doors from the end, Room 226. I can barely contain my excitement, as I head down the hall, trying not to rush and draw attention to myself. When I reach her room, her door is open, and she's seated in a wheelchair with her back to me, looking out the window.

I set my bag down against the wall and walk towards her.

"Mrs. Delaney?" There's a smile in my voice.

She doesn't respond, so I repeat myself a little louder. She turns then and looks at me. She looks the same, but she has aged since I last saw her. But just seeing her face

makes my heart warm. I lean over and hug her, she pats
my back.

"How are you? How have you been? I'm so glad I've
found you!" I crouch in front of her, taking her hands in
mine.

She speaks softly, with a smile, "Well I've been just
fine...but pardon me dear, I don't know who you are."

Her words hit me hard. I'm taken aback and stand up,
letting go of her hands, sitting on the edge of the bed
beside her.

"Mrs. Delaney, it's me Annie. Don't you remember me?"

She tilts her head to the side and looks at me for a
moment, I can see the concentration in her face, trying to
make the connections in her brain.

"I'm sorry dear, I don't know who you are." She's still
smiling, she's happy for the company, even if she doesn't
know why I'm here.

My heart is broken. She's here in front of me, and yet at the same time, she is a million miles away. I've found her, only to lose her all over again. I had so much that I wanted to tell her, needed to tell her, questions I needed to ask her. Did she know about Uncle Mink, what he did to me? Was she keeping the secret too?   Most of all, I wanted to thank her for being my saving grace in a world that was not kind to me. She fed me and cared for me, and did more to help me than my own mother ever did - and I never did get a chance to properly tell her how I felt. Only when I left her, did I realize how invaluable she really was in my life.

I try to explain to her who I am and she nods and smiles, but she's not really there. I try to jog her memory any way I can, telling her stories about when I was young, when Upsy and I would visit her, how Upsy loved to chase the chickens around her yard. She laughs then, saying incredulously, "Chickens?" She remembers none of it. But I keep trying, I tell her about Freddie, reminded her that Upsy died...anything and everything to make her see me. I repeated my name over and over again. She listened to all of it politely, but the Mrs. Delaney I knew is gone.

A nurse walks in then, smiling at both of us. She's here to take Mrs. Delaney's vital signs, as she does several times a day. Mrs. Delaney seems to be well looked after here. The nurse asks me how I know her, as she does her job. I tell her she was more than a neighbour when I was young – she was a substitute grandmother. A tear slips out when I mention that she doesn't seem to remember me anymore, and that makes me so sad. The nurse puts her stethoscope around her neck and pats my arm. She tells me that Mrs. Delaney's memory has gone downhill quite quickly over the past year. She has an aggressive form of dementia, which is taking its toll. Sometimes she has brief moments of clarity, but these are few and far between now. She's sorry that I have come to find her like this. I am too. The nurse leaves and I sit a few moments longer, both of us looking out the window quietly.

Finally I sigh and stand up. I might as well leave. I can't do anything more here. At least I got to see her, hug her, say some of the things I wanted to say – even if they fell upon deaf ears. I say goodbye and hug her one more time, telling her to take care, then I turn to leave.

As I pick up my bag off the floor, I hear her speak.

"I remember the chickens."

I turn back and she's nodding, a slight tremor in her hands
as she holding them out in front of herself.

I take them in mine, "You do?" I smile, filled with joy for
this small miracle.

She nods and then says, "Annie," with a contented,
knowing smile on her face.

And I know in that instant, for that one brief moment, she
is here.

But as soon she was, she is gone.

But that's all I needed. I hug her again and whisper, "I
love you," in her ear. Then I leave her room, turning
around just once in the doorway to hold this moment in

my heart just a second longer.

VI

So now I'm back on the bus. All my business is done, all my ghosts are put away; it's time to go forward. I take a moment and wonder what Upsy would be like today – at 18 years old. I bet she'd be beautiful and strong...she'd have grown out of her shy, awkward stage. She'd still be the same kind and caring friend I used to know...she'd still be my anchor and my lifeline. And she would still believe in me. I will do this for her. I won't let her down.

The miles roll on, as the bus rolls through Kansas, then Colorado, heading further and further West. I'm getting closer and closer to my new life – to my dreams. Everything is going to change now. I smile and look out the window, watching the world go by. So much has happened in my life, the years were long and often filled with pain, but I've come full circle. I'm starting a new life now, one that I'm creating for myself. I'm not living Mother's life anymore, and I have no intention on returning to the East Coast. I never want to set foot in her

house ever again. I need to succeed... I *need* to succeed.
It will be devastating if I don't.

<u>Epilogue</u>

Now do you see? Now do you realize why I never should have been a mother? Do you understand why I had to run...and what made me run? The ghosts of my childhood chased me, followed me everywhere, in my thoughts, in my dreams...I was only trying to get away from them. They haunted me in quiet moments, they made me feel that I would never have peace, that I deserved to be punished.

 You know the rest of my story... it's all laid out in black and white; all the rest of my sins and reprehensible actions told by my daughter, as I entangled her in the rest of my dysfunctional life. I condemned her to a prison of heartache; involving her in my search for...myself...which I never found after all. And I failed her profoundly - just as I had been failed over and over again. I became that which I loathed so deeply.

I thought I could do it - I wanted to have the happy, normal life that I saw all around me...but I just couldn't achieve it. When I met my husband, I thought it was serendipity that we were both originally from Missouri and I could go back home after all those years. I thought things would get better, life would be good. I don't know if I really ever loved him, but only because I never knew what love was. It was doomed to fail.

Life isn't easy for everyone. Some of us are born into a storm and continue to struggle, never catching a break. Some of us are able to break free of our horrible childhoods, but some of us aren't. We are so irreparably damaged, that we will never be normal.

I continued to see Upsy in my dreams from time to time throughout the rest of my life. She doesn't scare me anymore, but it does make me so sad, eliciting long forgotten thoughts, regrets and emotions that I never want to feel again. So I make myself go numb, so I can't feel anything. It's the only way I can cope with life, numb myself to it all; feel nothing, love no one ever again...and it works so well, that I can't even love my own family, let alone myself.

I hope you understand my story and forgive me for not being able to stop the legacy I inherited, for bequeathing it to someone who never deserved such pain. The sins of the mother pass onto the daughter...

About the author: Crazy cat lady, purveyor of laughs (sometimes tears), sarcasm expert, devoid of patience, sufferer of road rage, reader, writer, chef, mom , wife, legend ;) Born in 1971, resided in small town Ontario, moved to bigger town Ontario. Obtained a degree in Sociology and a grown up job somewhere in between. Content, happy and at peace with the world (for the most part). Finally.

Books can be ordered by request at
tmac_71@hotmail.com.